I0732492

ROYAL
Relations

EMILY SILVER

TRAVELIN' HOOSIER BOOKS

Copyright © 2022 by Emily Silver

All rights reserved.

This is a work of fiction. Names, characters, places and incidents are either the product of the author's imagination or are use fictitiously. Any resemblance to actual persons, living or dead, businesses, companies, events or locations is entirely coincidental.

No part of this book may be reproduced in any form or by any electronic or mechanical means, including information storage and retrieval systems, without written permission from the author, except for the use of brief quotations in a book review. For more information, please email the author at authoremilysilver@gmail.com.

Cover Design by Kari March Designs

Editing by Happily Editing Anns

www.authoremilysilver.com

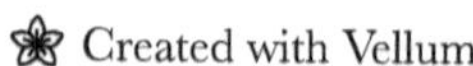 Created with Vellum

A Note from the Author

Thank you so much for reading Royal Relations! I have taken some literary license when writing this book in regard to the Succession to the Crown Act, passed in 2013. Prior to 2011, any second-born male could displace an older sister in line to the throne. Since this is my own royal world, this does not apply in this series.

Happy reading!

Prologue

CHARLOTTE

"You made it!" Ellie wraps her arms around me as I rush into the sitting room at the palace.

"Sorry I'm late. Lost track of time working."

"I'm just happy you were able to come." Ellie loops her arm through mine and pulls me farther into the crowded room.

"I thought you said this was going to be a small celebration."

Ellie rolls her eyes. "Sean's mum planned everything, and then my mum sort of took over."

"As she does. But it does look pretty good in here."

Flowers decorate all the surfaces in the family room in the palace. A table is overflowing with gifts in the corner. "Presents? I thought you didn't want any."

I turn my gaze back to Ellie. Her pink hair is braided around her head. She's wearing a long, white dress that clings to her baby bump. She's absolutely glowing.

"I didn't. Sean and I need nothing, but everyone brought something." Ellie's eyes shift to find Sean. He's standing next to someone I haven't seen before, but the stranger's eyes pull me in. Bright blue eyes that are filled with laughter. White teeth hidden behind plump lips.

"Who is that—" I'm cut off.

"Charlotte. I'm so pleased you could join us today." Aunt Katherine, better known as the Queen, pulls me in for a hug.

"I just can't believe Ellie is having a baby." I squeeze Ellie's shoulder. As cousins near the same age, she's been one of my closest friends for as long as I can remember. "I can't wait to meet this little baby."

"I just wish we knew what she was having." Katherine gives Ellie a look.

"Mum. You'll meet them soon enough," Ellie reminds her.

"Katherine. Stop bothering Eleanor." My mum appears at my side. "Hello, darling."

"Hi, Mum." I give her a quick side hug as a server with champagne walks by.

"Just you wait until Charlotte begins having kids. It will drive you just as crazy."

I choke over my sip of champagne at Aunt Katherine's words. "I'm not even dating someone. Let's not talk about that."

"Better you than me," Ellie laughs.

"I'm sure they'll be asking when baby number two will pop out before long."

The mystery man crosses my view, talking to James and Zara. My mum and Aunt Katherine get carried away into a conversation about the baby and who will have another child first. A conversation only mums can have.

"Who's that talking with James and Zara?" I whisper over the top of my drink to Ellie. No need to broadcast who I'm looking at.

"Who, Pierce? That's Sean's brother."

It's as if he hears his name. Pierce turns and looks over at Ellie and me. A small smile plays on his lips. Flutters erupt deep in my belly, something I haven't felt in a long time.

Before I can make my way over to him, my attention is pulled away and he's gone.

I need to meet this man.

Chapter One

CHARLOTTE

"I'm sorry, Your Highness, but it's just not possible."

I give my advisor, Jasper, a blank stare. "Why is wanting to create a charity to help women not possible?" I keep my voice even.

"The Queen thought it would step on too many toes." Jasper doesn't give me a passing glance as he moves to the next item on today's agenda. "You have lunch with the new Canadian ambassador next week, and tomorrow—"

"I'm sorry." I throw my hand out to stop him. "What does she mean by that?"

"Only that your proposal to start a new women's charity covers too much." His voice is dismissive. He's not even looking at me.

"Can you get more information?"

Jasper gives me a piercing look. I guess that answers that question. I don't hear another word of what's said. Wanting to help women would step on too many toes? Cover too much? I fight the eye roll that wants to come with being told no. It seems like anything I try to do these days is met with resistance.

Being in my position is a privilege, and one I don't take lightly. I love being able to do the work I do. But lately, it's been draining. Wanting to start my own charity to help women is something I'm passionate about. It's frustrating that I'm shot down with little explanation.

A knock on the door pulls my attention away from Jasper. "Excuse me. Can I steal Charlotte away?" Zara's head pops in through the door.

"Absolutely. Thank you for your time, Jasper. I hope you'll get me more information from the Queen, as this is something I want to pursue." I give him a withering stare, but it gets me nowhere.

"Thank God. I was in need of a rescue," I say as soon as we're out of my office. I link my arm through Zara's. "And why are my services required today?"

I'm nearly a head shorter than Zara, even in heels. I loved my cousin James's fiancée, Zara, immediately. With his twin, Ellie, renouncing her place in line to the throne, it's nice to have someone in the battlefield with me. If you want to call it that.

"James ended up going to Wales for the day for an event for Sporting Kids and left wedding tastings to me."

"Well, his loss is my gain. Are we tasting desserts?"

Zara laughs as we make our way down to the kitchens. We both have offices here at the palace. With James taking over more responsibility, he wanted Zara close by. Since we all work together, my office was moved here as well. It's nice to get to see her as often as I do.

"Please. The cake has been decided on for months. Apparently that takes much more skill than cooking the meal. We're tasting our dinner options today."

I shrug. "Still better than what I had planned for the rest of the afternoon."

We make our way down to the study overlooking the

gardens where lunch is being served. The kitchen staff is already bustling around, making sure everything is perfect.

"Your Highness. I didn't realize you'd be joining us." The head chef curtsies to me.

"James is otherwise busy today, so I figured it'd be helpful to have a second opinion."

"Excellent, Lady Zara. I'll bring over the first option and get your wine pairings."

"Remind me to thank James the next time I see him." My day had been droning on. Seeing the good work that James and Zara are doing with their charities makes me want to carve out my own space in the world. I don't want to be content doing what the Queen hands me, but it appears that's all I'm good for.

"Seems you could use a good distraction," Zara states matter-of-factly as the wine is poured and dishes are set before us with a flourish.

"For our starter, we have two options. Your guests may choose between marinated salmon, crab, and langoustines served atop a fresh herb salad, and quenelles served in a lobster sauce. Both pair well with the Sauvignon Blanc that you have now."

I nod to the waiter as he scurries away. "Cheers, Zara."

The wine is refreshingly crisp on this dreary London day. "Just what I needed," Zara remarks. "Now, tell me why you need distracting."

"God, this food is the perfect distraction. This salad is incredible," I moan around the tongs of my fork. The marinade on this salmon is delicious.

Zara gives me her teacher look. The one that used to scare her students into obeying her every word.

"I was told no on my charity idea."

Zara slumps back in her chair, taking a large sip of wine. "She said no?"

I nod. "All I got from Jasper is that I was trying to cover too much."

"You want to help too many people?" Her voice is as angry as I feel. "That's a load of bollocks."

I snort into my glass. "You are starting to sound just like James."

A blush creeps over Zara's face. "What can I say? He does rub off on you."

If I didn't like Zara so much, I'd be jealous of the happiness she's found with James. I thought I'd found my happily ever after with my last boyfriend, Michael, but he couldn't stand the spotlight. It's been two years of going to events on my own and seeing all my friends from uni fall in love and get married.

Not as if that's the only thing I want in my life. But lately, it seems that something is missing. I was hoping this charity would fill that void, but even that is a closed door for me.

"Would you want to help me with my patronage?" Zara spears a piece of crab into her mouth. "Oh my God. This is incredible. This is definitely going on the menu."

"I would fight you if you didn't include it." I sigh, taking a sip of my wine. "But no, I don't want to be a part of your charity. You and James are already doing such good work. I was hoping to have something of my own that could do the same."

Zara leans across the table, taking my hand in hers. "But you already are doing good work. The people love you. Do you know I was most scared that I couldn't live up to you?"

"That's just crazy." I shake my head, taking another sip of wine.

"It's true. I know Ellie was first in line, but the people love you. Don't sell yourself short."

This is why I love Zara. She's one of the kindest, most caring people I know, and I couldn't be happier for her and James.

Servers come to clear our plates, and the chef brings out the next course.

"For the first meal option, we have a Chardonnay paired with a lobster mousse stuffed chicken with seared asparagus on the side. Please make note of anything you like or don't like, and we can adapt the food accordingly."

Zara clinks her fresh glass to mine. "Have you thought of maybe trying to focus more on women in the charities you do currently have?"

I shake my head as I take a large bite of the chicken in front of me. "How does the kitchen come up with these meals? I'd gain a stone in a week if I ate such decadent food every day."

"I let them have free rein. If it were up to me, James and I would get married in our backyard, but that can't happen."

"You know you'll be the most beautiful bride there is. I can't wait to see your dress."

A smile lights up Zara's face. "Oh, Charlotte. I really do love it. I thought I would hate having to choose a specific designer, but I fell in love the moment I saw the dress." She points her fork at me. "Nice try trying to distract me."

I sip my wine, giving her a coy look over the glass. "I thought I had you. Most of my charities right now don't really apply to women. I wish I could make them, but they focus on kids, and I love those too much to give them up."

"Well, I don't think you should stop trying. Just because the Queen says no, does that really mean no?"

Zara and I lock eyes before laughter bubbles out of both of us. "Good one, Zara."

The chef is back at our side. "For the second meal option, we have a rich Cabernet Sauvignon served with lamb and seasonal vegetables."

Zara and I chat, passing the time during each tasting. By the time the third course comes out, Zara and I are giddy from the wine.

"Will we get to have all this wine with dinner?"

"You know we can't!" Zara says on a hiccup.

"It would make the day that much more enjoyable."

"It's going to be enjoyable because I get to marry James and then we can shag all we want because we're living together." Zara's laughter is masked by her hand going to her mouth. "Oh, bugger. I didn't mean to say that."

"Things I don't want to hear."

"I'll gladly hear all about yours once you find a beautiful man to bed." She clinks her glass a little too hard against mine. "What about Oliver? You could fancy him."

I try to keep in the laugh, but it's hard. "Ollie, James's friend from uni? Are you serious? I wouldn't touch him in a hazmat suit. He's worse than James."

Zara winces, and I speak quickly to apologize. "Sorry. I'd kill to have someone look at me the way James looks at you." James was the biggest playboy of all not long ago. But now, he's the happiest I've ever seen him with Zara.

"Much better. Don't worry. I'm determined to find you a proper man."

I can only shake my head.

It'd be easier finding Neverland than a man who would want to take on the royal life.

"Thanks, Zara, but I think I'll pass."

"And what's your alternative? Moping around the palace? You look miserable."

I stab the remainder of the lamb on my plate. "Gee, thanks. Just what every girl wants to hear."

"Sorry, but have you ever considered taking a break? You look exhausted. I know you've been pushing yourself since Ellie renounced her spot in line to the throne."

"As much as I would love a holiday, I could never get one right now. Not after the way Ellie left."

Zara gives me a shocked look. "You mean they wouldn't just let anyone run away again?"

Laughter bubbles out of me, bringing me out of my sombre mood. "I guess you'll just have to make do with having me and my mopey self around."

"Well, if it means I get to drink wine and eat indulgent food with you throughout the day, then I'll keep you around."

Shoreditch
INK

Chapter Two

"Goal!" Liam runs around the pitch, pumping his arms.

"What the fuck, Hunter?" I glare at our goalie. "My grandmum could have blocked that shot."

He flips me the bird. "Why don't you come play goalkeeper and then we'll see just how good you are."

"Got your knickers in a twist because you're losing?" Liam drapes his arm over my shoulder.

I shove him off. "Just you wait. We'll come back and finish you off."

"I'd like to see you try, Davies." He jogs back to the centre of the pitch, getting ready to take the ball.

Fucker. Liam comes at me dribbling the ball. He tries to fake me out, but I don't bite. I steal the ball from him and take off down the field, his cursing following behind me.

On a breakaway, I don't hesitate to shoot. The goalie has no chance of blocking my shot as it sails into the back of the net.

"Fuck, yeah!" My team is cheering on the sidelines.

"You're acting like you just won the World Cup for England." Bitterness coats Liam's voice.

"Oh, I'm sorry. Are you being a sore loser?" I mock a whiny voice to him.

Liam and I have been playing football together for years. We met during a pick-up game and have been best mates ever since.

"Don't get so cocky over there. Still plenty of time left in the game." Liam flips me off as we take our positions.

The game continues at a fast pace. Guys switch out on and off the pitch. It's a relaxed game. We don't have a lot of the same rules as the big leagues. We're just playing for the fun of it. I've met some of my best mates out here.

The ball bounces back to me, but I lose control, nearly wiping out when Liam comes out of nowhere.

"You fucker!" I yell, chasing him down the pitch. He gets an easy shot on goal, but Hunter blocks it with ease.

"Yes! Take that!" I give him a shove as I go to congratulate Hunter. He sails the ball out of the box towards the other end of the field.

"Get your head in the game, Davies. We need to beat these arseholes." He pushes me back into the game, and I can only shake my head at him.

God, I love being out here with these guys. Whenever anything is going wrong in life, this is the distraction I need. Running around like a kid, playing the game I love.

"I CAN'T BELIEVE you wankers won," Liam chokes out into his beer. The local pub across from our small pitch is always our post-game hangout spot. Half the time, the waitresses comp our drinks.

"You're lucky we don't play for tattoos. Can you imagine inking Hunter's face on your arse?" I snort over my beer.

"Dude. That's not even funny." Horror mars his face.

"Anyone would be lucky to have this mug marked on them for life." Hunter, with his curly blond hair and bright blue eyes, could be a model. No one actually knows what he does.

"It'd scare my girl off anytime we fucked."

"Ahh, Liam. I think we've discovered the reason you don't have a girlfriend."

He pierces me with a questioning stare. "Because I'm so handsome, they would die of pleasure?"

"Because you're a wanker who says things like 'anytime we fucked.'"

Liam shrugs his shoulders. "I'm not ready to be tied down and become a miserable old sod. Too many beautiful women in London."

"You lads doing all right?" The waitress comes by, dropping off another round of drinks. Even though we didn't order them. This is why we keep coming back here.

"Doing better now that you're here." Liam winks at her.

"Don't piss where you eat, mate." I slap him upside the head.

She walks away, shaking her head. "What if she's my soulmate and you just ruined my chance with her?"

Hunter coughs out the gulp of beer he just took. "Don't make me laugh. If she's your soulmate, then I'll bloody be married to Princess Charlotte next year."

A bark of laughter escapes me. "Oh, like you could date a princess."

"Your brother managed to snag one."

"How my brother ever got a princess to fall in love with him, I'll never know."

Ellie, formerly Princess Eleanor, ran away from royal life and straight into my brother's tattoo shop. No one had any idea who she was. Dying one's hair pink tends to do that. But after Sean discovered who she was when her grandfather passed, she renounced her place in line for the throne and is now happily expecting a baby with my brother. I've never seen him so damn happy.

"If there's hope for him, there's hope for us all." Hunter raises his glass in cheers.

"Except Pierce. He's going to end up moving back to the country and living with his mummy."

"Fuck off, you wanker." I snag Liam's beer, draining it before he has the chance. "As much fun as hanging out with you lot is, I'm heading home. I've got an early appointment tomorrow."

"Aww, finally going to see a doctor about your tiny dick?" Hunter joins in on giving me shit now.

"Remind me why I'm friends with you?" I flip them both off, before slapping their backs. "See you next week for drinks?"

They raise their glasses as I head out into the cold London night.

"SO YOU LIKE THE DESIGN?" I show the cover-up piece I've been working on for the last week to the man in my chair. When the old guy came into the shop, he was looking for Sean, but got me instead. I shouldn't let it bother me like it does, but everyone always wants my brother. He runs one of the best tattoo shops in all of London. But sometimes, it feels like I'm playing second fiddle to him.

"Damn. You do some great work, kid. Are we good to get started?"

"Absolutely. This is going to look great."

I get to work, readying my station. For someone who feels like he gets lost in his brother's shadow, choosing to go into the same line of work as him was odd. But when Sean gave himself his first tattoo, I was hooked. I've been learning about the art of tattooing ever since.

And cover-ups have become my favourite. What people wanted at one point in their life and what they want now is always cool to see. Sometimes, I'm covering up some fucked-up shit. Other times, old girlfriends' names. I've even covered up a few mum tattoos. Those are always awkward.

"You coming over tonight?" Sean's voice pulls me away from the work at hand. The person I'm tattooing doesn't even notice. His heavy breaths tell me he's asleep. The big burly man has no qualms about needles. Looking at the clock, a few hours have gone by. This is why I love what I do. I can get lost in the work.

"Why do I need to come over tonight?" I wipe the excess ink away, tracing the needle over the stencil.

"Because Ellie and I need to talk to you."

"And if I have plans?"

He doesn't say anything until I glance up at him. His arms are crossed over his chest. "Cancel them. This is important."

I huff out a breath, pulling the needle away from the body laid out before me. "Fucking hell. I'll say yes if you piss off and let me work."

"Ouch, someone's in a grouchy mood," Trevor pipes up from the booth beside me. Christ. I love working with these two guys, but some days they wear me out.

"Why are you in such a mood?" Sean leans against the wall of my space in the studio. Sean doesn't want to hear about staying out too late after football. He's all loved up at home while some of us still enjoy hitting the pubs.

"Would you two leave him alone?" Pink shoos them away. Her bright pink hair, hence the nickname, is plaited over one shoulder. Trevor goes back to his own work while Sean lingers over Ellie. She's seven months pregnant, and he worries over her. She shoves him away. "Sorry about your brother."

"Not sure why he's got his knickers in a twist about dinner tonight."

"Great design. Did you draw it yourself?" Ellie draws attention away from Sean, gazing down at my work.

"Of course I did. Only the best."

"Will you please come to dinner for me?" She bats her eyelashes at me.

Any fight I had leaves my body. "You know I can't say no to you, Pink."

Her eyes sparkle. "Fab. I promise, you won't regret it."

Shoreditch
INK

Chapter Three

PIERCE

"Pierce. You've made my night!" Ellie's bump greets me before she does, wrapping her arms around my shoulders.

"You're pretty hard to say no to." I drop a kiss on each cheek, hanging my coat on the rack. Ellie and Sean live in a posh neighbourhood near Shoreditch. While I thought it would be overly stuffy, Ellie has made it into a cosy home.

"Glad one of us could convince you to come over." Sean greets me with a beer.

"Will you stop being such an arse to your brother?" Ellie pleads with him, smacking him on the chest.

"You're lucky I like you so much." I give her a wink, as the door swings open behind me.

"Sorry. I'm not late, am I?" A curvy brunette slams into me. "Oh crap, sorry!" She rights herself on my chest, and a spark of heat moves through me.

"No problem. I'm Pierce, this wanker's brother." I extend my hand to her.

"Charlotte. Ellie's cousin." Her smile is bright, dark red

lipstick staining plump lips. This woman is gorgeous with her deep brown eyes the colour of molasses.

"Come inside before you freeze." Ellie pulls her in for a hug as best she can. The late fall air is colder than normal.

I can't take my eyes off this woman. I've always known who she was. Living in London, you can't escape the royals. But in the time I've known Ellie, I've never met Charlotte. Only saw her at the baby shower. Even though I didn't meet her, I was aware of her. Anyone in their right mind would be. She's fecking gorgeous.

"How was your day?" Ellie wraps an arm around her shoulder and drags her into the kitchen, but not before my eyes find hers. I give a small waggle of my eyebrows, my eyes fixed on her as she leaves the room.

"Things go better at the shop this afternoon?" Sean sips his beer, flopping down on the sofa in front of me.

"Once you lot let me get to work."

"I wasn't trying to bother you."

I sit next to my brother, kicking his leg with my foot. "Relax. I'm not mad."

At least, I'm not anymore. I love him. But growing up, I was always following in his footsteps. Teachers and coaches alike asked me why I couldn't be more like by brother. Sean was always considerate and thought everything through.

Me? I was always more rambunctious. Still am. Don't really think twice before making a decision. It's served me well, but sometimes, it makes me feel like I'm lacking.

"Your piece looks great. You'll have to show me how you did the cover-up on it."

My chest puffs out with pride. Sean rarely asks for help, but I love when he comes to me. "Who decides to get a skull and crossbones on a cupcake? It doesn't make the cupcake more badass."

"From your lips to God's ears. People get the weirdest shit tattooed on them."

"Keeps us in business." Sean tilts his beer bottle towards mine in agreement.

"Until then, we're here for all the weird shit people want," he says with a smirk.

"Okay, now that everyone is here"—Sean jumps up as soon as Ellie and Charlotte walk in the room—"we can tell you the reason we brought you both here tonight." I'm not sure which one of them is glowing more. The baby isn't even here, and Sean is beaming.

"Don't drag it out." Charlotte sits down on the loveseat next to me. Warmth radiates from her, causing chills to wrack my body. My palms start to sweat. Christ, I've barely said more than two words to this woman and I'm acting like an altar boy who's seen a girl for the first time.

"We wanted you both here tonight to ask you to be the godparents to our little one." Ellie's face is nervous. "You both mean so much to us, and we want our baby to have you both in their life."

Charlotte jumps up, screeching, as she rushes to Ellie. Tears are in both their eyes as they hug one another.

"You want me to be the godfather?" Shock colours my voice as I stand, making my way over to Sean.

"Is it that big of a shock?" He does a good job hiding the hurt.

"Sorry. It's just, fuck, I'm not a great influence, am I? Shit, do you really want your baby's first words being a curse word?" I run a hand through the scruff on my jaw. "Godfather? Really?"

"If anything happens to us, God forbid, there's no one else I want taking care of my kid. You'll be the best uncle and godfather, Pierce."

"Shit." Emotion chokes up my throat as I pull my

brother in for a hug. "I still can't believe you're going to be a dad."

He pulls back, looking over at Ellie, who's now staring at the two of us. "Fuck, I can't believe it myself. Would you have thought a couple of years ago that this would be happening?"

"That the princess would fall madly in love with you and leave her life behind for you? I'd say you were bloody well pissed."

"You're such a dick." He wraps an arm around my neck, pulling me down and rubbing my head.

"Oh, very mature, Dad."

"Okay, boys. Sean, come help me with dinner. Let's leave our godparents to get to know one another." Ellie winks, pulling Sean behind her. He goes willingly. He would follow her to the ends of the world. And damn, if that doesn't make me jealous. I want to follow after someone like my brother does.

Charlotte

GODMOTHER. Joy threatens to bubble out of me as I stare at the handsome man in front of me. "Can you believe we're going to be godparents?" I clap my hands in front of me.

"I can't believe my brother is going to be a dad. Like who decided we're ready for that responsibility?"

"There's actually a class you take. Parenting 101. Ways to not completely screw up raising your kid."

He quirks a brow at me. "Aren't you the funny one."

"Better than having any other labels." I plop down on the sofa next to Pierce. His sculpted chest and arms fill out his jumper. He props an ankle over his knee, his thighs bunching as he settles back into the sofa cushions.

"Fight a lot of stigma as a princess?" Pierce sips his beer, the liquid glistening on his lips. With bright blue eyes and dark brown hair that has me itching to run my fingers through it, Pierce is one of the sexiest men I've seen in a long while. Not that I've been looking. Ever since my ex left me, it's been hard to find anyone willing to take on this life.

"Just have to toe the line."

"Seems like you 'toe the line' just fine." He makes air quotes around the line I just gave him.

"Just because I'm a princess doesn't mean I don't rebel in my own ways. I'm not an idiot like my cousin James was, but there's more to me than meets the eye."

"Okay. If you don't toe the line, what's one of your most embarrassing moments?"

"Most embarrassing moment?" I tap my lips with my finger.

"You can't have that many embarrassing moments, can you?" Pierce's handsome face is puzzled, with pursed lips, eyes wide in wonderment.

"It's hard to tell you who it's more embarrassing for, me or the First Lady of France."

He snorts. "Only you could have a story involving a head of state from another country."

"You asked what the most embarrassing thing to happen to me was." I quirk a brow at him. "I was visiting France on behalf of my grandfather, and I was attending a state dinner with the president. They were welcoming me at their home when I tripped on the cobblestones and ended up falling into the First Lady."

Pierce winces, sipping on his beer. "This can't be good."

I nod my head. "I ended up grabbing her chest and ripping her gown. It was plastered all over the French news by the end of the night. Said I was trying to start war with France."

"A war?"

"They were all very dramatic about it. Thankfully, she didn't flash anyone. I was utterly mortified, but the First Lady was very kind."

"And you didn't start a war with France. Cheers to that." Pierce clinks his beer bottle against my wine glass. An easygoing smile spreads across his lips. He looks like he's up to no good. I should turn and run in the other direction, but for the first time in a long while, someone isn't talking to me like I'm the princess, but just a regular woman. It's refreshing.

"What's your most embarrassing moment?" I ask, sipping on my wine.

"I got pantsed at a football match once." Pierce doesn't hesitate.

I nearly choke over my sip of wine. "You play football?" My eyes peruse his body. He doesn't look like a footballer.

"A few mates and I play together every few weeks. We're hardly the national team, but it's fun."

"And getting pantsed while playing is fun?"

Pierce chuckles to himself, setting his now empty beer bottle on the coffee table in front of us.

"It's fucking awesome. I mean, not the getting pantsed part. My mate did it to steal the ball from me. Flashed everyone."

His laughter is contagious. "This doesn't really sound embarrassing to me."

"Eh. Could've been worse. Just us taking the piss on the pitch."

I roll my eyes at him. "So just boys being boys."

"Hey!" Pierce shoves my shoulder. "It's a very spirited match, and we all play to win. It's very serious."

"Oh, yes, I'm sure it is. And what do you win if you win the match?" I sit on my knees, moving closer to Pierce. Something about him draws me in. Scruff lines his square jaw as his eyes focus on me.

"Free drinks at the pub." Pierce says this like I should know.

"Who wouldn't want their drinks paid for?"

"How about I pay for your drinks sometime?" The easy way Pierce says this catches me off guard.

"Like a date?"

Pierce shifts closer to me, his knees bumping into mine. The small contact causes goose pimples to break out on my skin. "Yes, Charlotte." The way he says my name has heat licking up my spine as I lean farther into him. "When a man asks you out for drinks, typically that means it's a date."

"Smartass."

Pierce tucks a piece of hair behind my ear. His fingers linger. "What do you say? Date with the smartass?"

"A date it is."

I couldn't wipe the grin off my face if I tried.

Shoreditch

Chapter Four

PIERCE

Fuck me, she's beautiful. Charlotte is walking towards me, skin-tight jeans and a jumper hugging all her delicious curves. The early evening light makes her look like an angel. I don't know how I got her to agree to a date with me.

"Hey, handsome." She's got a swing to her hips as she walks towards me. Her red painted lips are bright with a smile.

"Hi." Words fail me. This woman is looking at me like I'm dessert. She's running her hands down my leather jacket. Only the best for Charlotte.

"So where are you taking me tonight?" She swings her hair over her shoulder, exposing the gentle slope of her neck. It takes everything I have not to bite down on the pulsing vein there. To trace my lips over the gentle thrum of her pulse.

"How does mini golf sound?" I pull her into my arms, loving the feel of her curves under me.

"Mini golf? I don't think I've ever played mini golf before." Her eyes are sparkling.

I can't keep the flirting out of my tone. "Well then, stick with me, love, and I'll show you a good time."

"A good time, huh?" Charlotte wraps her arms around my neck, playing with the hair at the nape of my neck. "You think you can show me a good time?"

This time, I don't hesitate. I capture those red lips with mine—those alluring, pouty lips. She licks my lips and I open to her. Bloody hell. This is hot. Charlotte is taking control of this kiss, and I'm at her mercy as she leans farther into me. My hands drift lower, settling just above her perfect arse, and pull her closer to me, sinking deeper into this kiss. I could stay right here all night, wrapped up with her.

"Fuck, Charlotte." The wind blows her hair around us, as I tuck it behind her ear. Her cheeks are red, her lips swollen. All I want to do is toss her over my shoulder and go back to my flat. But I have the perfect date in mind. Something away from the spotlight that I'm sure she's going to love.

"C'mon. Show me where this amazing place is." She takes my hand in hers, walking backwards. I'm helpless to do anything but follow.

"SWINGERS? Should I really be at a place called Swingers?" I can see the question lingering in her eyes.

"I promise, I'm not going to pimp you out to someone who doesn't deserve you." Fuck, I don't even think I deserve her, but here I am.

I push the door open, and we're swept away to a different world. Flowers line the wall near the bar, as music plays throughout the old warehouse. Colorful plants, wind-mills, and all sorts of contraptions line the holes.

A few eyes turn to Charlotte, but her security officers wave them off. I guess I've gotten used to them since Ellie still has them. The last thing I want is for her face to be splashed all over the headlines, but her smile at me says she doesn't have a care in the world.

"So, you going to teach me how to play?" She grabs the scorecard from my hand.

"Not sure how much I'll be teaching you. I'm not the best at this either."

Charlotte sidles up to me. "Well then, best start stretch-ing, because I'll teach you a thing or two."

She winks as she walks over to the bar. Bloody hell. I say a silent prayer that no one can see the semi I'm now sporting. Charlotte is unlike any girl I've ever met. I've only known her a few days, but I know she's different. Whereas Ellie shied away from the spotlight, Charlotte has no problem being in it.

"What'll ya have?" the bartender asks, not looking twice at Charlotte.

"Moscow mule for me, and…" she trails off.

"Same."

I lean against the bar, watching as she turns into me. "So how'd you find this place?"

The bartender slides our drinks across the bar and goes back to the couple now in front of her. I take a long pull on the drink. Damn, that's good. "A client told me about it. Said his boyfriend loved coming here because he feels like Alice."

"Alice?"

"Alice in Wonderland."

Charlotte looks around the space. "I see it. Let's go see if we can wander down the rabbit hole."

She grabs my hand and leads me in the direction of the first hole. Setting my drink down, I grab two putters and balls from the stand behind us. I hand Charlotte hers, our fingers grazing. It sends a zing of electricity moving through me. Fuck. This woman does things to me that no other woman has done before. And judging by the look on her face, she feels it too.

"Alright, ladies first." I gesture for her to go. A Ferris wheel sits at the end of the hole. Flowers line the bricks on either side of the fake turf. The lights are low overhead.

"Okay." She takes a readying sip of her drink, and hands it to me. She sets her ball down and takes her stance. The wiggle of her hips is intoxicating. So intoxicating I miss seeing her hit the ball.

"Hey, not bad!" she cheers, reaching for a high five.

"Beginner's luck." I smirk at her, taking a sip of her drink. I eye her as she watches me.

"So we're sharing a drink now?"

She walks up to me, taking a drink right where my lips were. Who is this woman? How did I get so lucky to find her?

"Figured I'd get some of your good luck." I drop a kiss on her cheek as I set up my shot.

"Your hips are all wrong. And the way you're holding the club isn't how it's done."

My eyes meet hers. It's as if we're the only two people here. "And since when did you become a world expert in golf?"

"Since I can do this." Charlotte moves to stand behind me and angles my hips. I doubt either of us know what we're doing, but I don't care. "I think that works much better, don't you think?" She squeezes my side and moves away as I hit the ball into the wall. It bounces off, landing only a short ways away from where I started.

"Christ, you're not playing fair, woman." I give her my best hard look. But the smile on her face would melt even the world's hardest person.

"Never said I would." She hops by me on her way to take her next shot. It's going to be a long night.

Charlotte

"THAT'S NOT FAIR. You can't drop your ball in the hole and say you win the hole." My hands are fisted on my hips as I stare at Pierce. We've been cheating all night. We aren't playing by the rules, and I love it.

"What are you going to do about it?" I have half a mind to walk right up to him and kiss that smug smile off his face, but we're in a crowded area of the club. As much as I want to kiss him, I don't want it splattered all over the news. Damn paparazzi taking pictures of every single thing.

Instead, I play dirty.

I walk right up to him, my eyes at his shoulders. Even in my heeled booties, I'm still shorter than he is. "If we weren't in the middle of a crowded area, I'd kiss the everloving piss out of you. Make you so dizzy with need that you couldn't see straight, so I'd win the next five holes."

"Only five?" His voice is gruff with need. I've hit my intended target.

I graze my fingers up his chest. "There's only five left." I walk off to the next hole. "You coming or what?"

His growl hits my ears as I approach the next hole. It's

tucked behind a wall. A flower-lined pergola sits over the hole.

Pierce's heat overwhelms me as he stands at my side. "You think you're going to get away with that?"

"Pretty sure I already did." I'm not looking at him. My focus is on the pergola ahead of me. Pierce's lips land on my neck, just below my ear.

It takes everything I have not to let out a groan. The scruff on his face does things to me that I shouldn't be thinking in public. This is getting out of hand and getting out of hand fast.

"What are you waiting for? Going to take the shot?"

His voice sends shivers down my spine. The ball hits the short wall on the course and bounces up and over, clanking off the metal walls of the building.

"What a shame." Pierce steps back, and I lament the loss of his heat. "Time to learn from the master."

I stalk off to grab my ball as Pierce takes his shot, directly into the pergola and in the hole.

"Holy shit!" he yells, grabbing me around the waist and swinging me around, all earlier jabs forgotten. "I aced it! World's best mini-golfer right here."

My laughter is bubbling out of me as he sets me down and lays a kiss on my cheek. "You really are good luck for me, Charlotte."

"Next time just taunt me the entire time, and then you'll ace it on the fourteenth hole."

"I'd be annoyed at that, but I got a hole in one! I should sign up to play golf with the professionals." He struts to the hole to grab his ball.

"Pretty sure the professionals don't act like this when they get a hole in one."

"You're right. They're probably way worse and throw

their clubs into the water. But seeing as how we're in the middle of London, we'll get dinner to celebrate."

"Sounds fab."

Pierce drapes his arm over my shoulders as we walk to the next hole. "And since you're the loser, you must buy."

Now I'm laughing for a whole other reason. "I'd say you're so full of shit that you should buy dinner, but I can't even help it. I'll buy you whatever you want."

I CAN'T REMEMBER the last time I've had so much fun on a first date. Or any date for that matter. Most people tend to steer clear of anything that might be too public, with me being a princess and all. Pierce found us a private booth in the back for dinner and drinks. After going through the entire course, it's nice to be away from prying eyes.

"We might have to come back here and try again." I grab a street taco and take a bite. I'd say I kicked Pierce's arse, but that would mean I did well. Neither of us has much game.

"We'll have to set a wager next time." He takes a long drink of his beer, not turning his eyes from mine. They're blue like the sea. So deep, I could get lost in them.

"You know royalty can't gamble." I give him my best smirk. His eyes find my lips this time. What I wouldn't give to kiss him again. He has the softest lips. So sensual that it's hard to keep my mind off them. I want a repeat—any chance I can get.

"I didn't say we'd be doing it with money." His eyes are heated with lust. It drives me mad.

"Oh yeah?" I slide closer to him in the booth. It's quiet

back here. My security officers are close by, so I know we're okay here. "What do you have in mind?"

"I was thinking something like this." His lips take mine in a soft kiss. He tastes like the beer he was drinking. He pulls back slightly, and it's like my lips are magnets to his. I follow, the butterflies in my belly not wanting to lose this contact with him.

I slide my hand up the soft fabric of Pierce's shirt, wrapping my hand around his neck. I capture his lips, teasing them with my tongue. His groan grants me access to his mouth. My ex used to hate that I liked to take control when kissing, but there's something so powerful about it. It turns me on. And Pierce gives it to me.

The soft velvet of his tongue has my core tightening with need. It takes everything I have not to move into his lap and rock my hips over him. He breaks the kiss, lips moving along my jaw, back to my ear.

"Bloody hell, Charlotte. We can't keep doing this, or you'll be in the papers tomorrow." I have to bite back my groan. All I want to do is go home with Pierce. I'm a woman who knows what she wants. And right now, I want Pierce. If only I wasn't a princess and could act on this desire flowing through me.

"I wish this was like any first date, and we could go home together." I drop my forehead to his.

"Thank God we have a table to hide how hard you're making me right now."

I giggle at his words. "Pretty sure that could be said of how you've been feeling all night."

A pinch at my side has me throwing my head back in laughter.

"Sorry I'm not more of a gentleman."

"Someone who isn't a gentleman wouldn't admit that." I trace my fingers over his swollen lips. This is bad. I think

I could fall for Pierce. With his intense blue eyes, innocent face, and those tattoos. I never thought I'd be a woman who enjoyed tattoos, but on Pierce? I want to learn every intimate detail about each of them. Trace them with my fingers. With my tongue.

Pierce is lighting a fire in me that I long thought was dead. After Michael left, it felt like there was something wrong with me. That no matter what I did, no one would be able to love all sides of me, both the private side and the very public side. Everyone says they're okay with my position, but once they face that public side, they sing a different tune.

But Pierce didn't shy away from it. Instead of taking me on a palace-approved date, he brought me to my new favourite spot in London. Who knew mini golf could be such a turn-on?

And the man who brought me here is fast turning into my new favourite person.

Chapter Five

CHARLOTTE

The grin on my face has been plastered there since this morning. I can't remember the last time I've had such a good first date. A fun first date. I keep trying to rework the charity idea I have, to be better suited to talk about with the Queen again, but my thoughts keep drifting back to Pierce.

To the way his eyes lit up when he first saw me. And the excitement in his voice when we went mini golfing. Who knew mini golf could be so much fun?

And that kiss? I still feel it, all the way down to my toes. Nothing can wipe the smile off my face today.

"Your Highness. The Queen will be in shortly to discuss a few matters with you." My advisor dips low before leaving the room.

Damn. It's never good if she wants an impromptu meeting. But maybe this will be a good chance to discuss the new charity I want to start. She's been rather evasive anytime I want to speak with her.

"Charlotte. How are you today?" Aunt Katherine, or

Queen Katherine as most call her, sweeps into the room in a bubble of floral perfume and a finely pressed suit.

"I'm well. And you?" I give her the customary double kiss, cheek greeting before sitting back down. Nerves are fluttering in my belly.

"I want to talk to you about this boy you're seeing."

"Pierce?"

She nods. "Sean's brother, no?"

"Yes. We had dinner at Sean and Ellie's the other night. He was here for the baby shower."

"And then you proceeded to have a date?" She sets a few magazines down in front of me. There, plastered all over the pages of gossip rags, are images of Pierce and me on our date. Anger churns inside me. I hate that we can't have a normal first date. Even being third in line, every move I make is documented for the entire world to see. It hasn't been as bad with the pending royal wedding, but they always find me.

"We weren't doing anything wrong." There's a defensiveness in my tone. Pictures of Pierce standing behind me, hands on my hips, while helping me swing, grace the pages of these magazines. Us having a drink. It's nothing that any other person wouldn't be doing on a first date.

"He's a bad influence, and we have a certain image to uphold as the royals of this nation. We can't be seen drinking and carrying on like this in public."

"Carrying on? It's not like we were having sex in the middle of the course for everyone to see!" I throw the magazines down and stand to match her. "It was two people having fun and getting to know one another."

"Be that as it may, you cannot see him again."

I rear back, as if she slapped me. "I'm sorry? I can't see him again?"

"With everything we go through with the press, I can't have another scandal coming down on us."

I cross my arms, levelling her with a stare. "And what makes you think there will be a scandal?"

"Ellie renounced her place in line to the throne for Sean. Look at what James and Zara are still going through."

"The press paid off their neighbours to get compromising photos of them!" I shout. Images of them having sex were leaked to the press. It was devastating. They almost broke up over it, but thank God they didn't.

"It's only a matter of time before something happens, and we can't handle another blow like that this early in my reign. I'm sorry, but no."

"And if I don't stop seeing him?" Every second of my life is already controlled. Every move monitored. Every place I go carefully vetted. Don't get me wrong, I love my life. I love getting to help and support the people in my country. But why can't I have one thing for myself?

"It's either the crown or him. And I know you'll make the right decision."

"That's it?" The air leaves my lungs on a huff.

"I will not discuss this any further, Charlotte." Her voice is clipped, ending the conversation. Anger boils up inside me as she spins on her heel to leave.

"Wait! Can I talk to you about the charity I want to start?"

She turns to face me, her lips pursed in a grim look. "Why are you still on that, Charlotte? I have set up plenty of events for you these next few weeks that are perfect for you."

"I'm sorry, you've set up events for me? Why am I just now hearing about this?"

"Your advisors were made aware. These events are much more conducive to helping the people of this country."

"Are women not people of this country? Do they not deserve our help?" I can't keep the ire from my voice.

"Charlotte." Her voice is stern. I'm not going to like what she says. "You have an idea, but it's too broad. I commend you for wanting to help the women of our nation, but you're wanting to do too much."

"What if I change it? Narrow my focus. Would you consider it then?"

"I would take it under advisement, but you are to continue with the events I've set up for you this week for our current patronages. Now, if you'll excuse me." She waves me off.

Aunt Katherine leaves the room without another backwards glance at me. My heart sinks at the thought of not seeing Pierce again. The few men I've seen these last few years were more interested in the crown than anything else. Trying to date with the weight of a crown hanging over your head is impossible.

But Pierce didn't think twice before asking me out. Sure, he knows Ellie and knows what she's dealt with in the past. All I can think of is how gutted he'll be when I tell him I can't see him again.

It was one date, but it was so different from anything I'd ever experienced. We had the best time together, and I don't want to lose out on that feeling.

Anger fuels me as I pick up the phone and dial someone who I hope can talk some sense into the Queen.

"Hi darling," my mum's voice rings.

"Mum. I need your help." Despite Mum marrying into the Ainsworth family, she's always been close to Aunt

Katherine. Thick as thieves back in the day, from what I heard.

"Everything okay?"

"Well, I met this man, and he is—" I don't even get to finish my sentence.

"You met someone? Where? Tell me the details." Mum's voice goes high with excitement.

"That's the problem. It's Sean's brother. And the Queen doesn't approve of him."

"Did she say why?"

"Only that he would be a bad influence on me."

"Maybe she's just trying to protect you."

"Protect me from what?"

"You know what the press can be like if someone doesn't fit the mold."

I want to scream. "Does it not matter what I want?"

"Darling,"—Mum's voice takes on a soft tone, but it sounds pitying—"just because you want someone, doesn't mean they are ready for royal life. I grew up the daughter of a duke, and it was an adjustment even for me."

"So because Aunt Katherine decides he'll be a bad influence, I don't even get the chance to see if we'll work out?"

She sighs, long and heavy. "Charlotte, this is between you and your aunt. I don't want to get involved and be put in the middle. I love you both, and I don't want to hurt either one of you."

Damn my mother for wanting to be so reasonable. I sigh. "You're right. I guess I'm just upset. I'll let you get back to work."

"Stop by for dinner this week, love."

"I will. Love you, Mum."

"Love you, darling."

I hang up the phone. Frustration over my situation surges through me. That smile that I was walking around with all morning is gone. First my charity and then Pierce? You've pissed off the wrong princess.

Shoreditch
INK

Chapter Six

PIERCE

I can't remember the last time I was nervous to have a woman over to my flat. When Charlotte called today to change our plans, nerves took over. This woman is a princess, for fuck's sake. Sure, our first date went off without a hitch, but we were on a level playing field. Now she's coming to my flat.

My flat is fine, if not on the small side. Artwork I've done over the years covers the walls. My bedroom barely fits a bed, and a small sofa takes up most of the living space. It's never bothered me before because it's exactly what I want. But when an actual princess is coming over? It's hard not to see the differences between us.

A knock at the door ratchets up my nerves. Swinging it open, I have to step aside as one of Charlotte's security officers sweeps inside. Charlotte's standing outside with another officer.

"Sorry about this. Standard protocol." A blush creeps up her face as they search my flat. No doubt she hates this as much as I do.

"All clear. We'll be waiting downstairs should you need

anything, Your Highness." They clear out as fast as they came in.

"Hi." Charlotte walks up to me, wrapping her arms around my waist. It calms the earlier panic that was rising inside of me.

"Hi, love." I squeeze her closer to me. The soft scent of her perfume wraps around me, setting me at ease. "Care for dinner?"

"Mm, it smells great in here. You cooked just for me?" She steps out of my arms, walking into the kitchen.

"Just for you." Charlotte lifts the lid off the pot, sticking her nose in the pot roast I'm making.

She turns her head, eyes wide and sparkling at me. "There is something very sexy about a man who knows how to cook."

"Oh yeah?" I step into her space. I haven't known her long, but I need to feel her under me. To feel her curves. To feel her soft skin. Need, need, need.

"Of course, you could be a terrible cook, and then we'll both be fucked."

Laughter escapes out of me as I bury my face in Charlotte's neck. "I'll have you know I'm an amazing cook."

"Whatever you say, Pierce." Fuck, I love the way my name rolls off her tongue. Sensual and sweet all at the same time. I grab the wine I picked up for us and pour us each a glass.

"Cheers." I clink my glass against hers as I take a steadying sip. Just being around this woman has my heart beating faster.

"So, why the change of venue this evening?" I plate our dinner, as Charlotte moves to the small table. She's wearing yoga pants and an oversized jumper. No makeup. She's absolutely stunning all the time, but even more beautiful when she's like this.

"Why don't we wait until after dinner? Not let it ruin the mood."

My skin prickles. Not ruin the mood? "Well, that's not going to put a downer on the evening." I set her plate of food in front of her and take the seat next to her. She's not looking at me but focusing too hard on her dinner.

Charlotte cuts herself a piece of meat, her delicate fingers holding her knife and fork the proper way. Her lips wrap around the fork, taking a bite. What I wouldn't give to be that fork right now as she moans around it.

"Pierce. That is so good." Her eyes are closed as she savours, and fuck, if that doesn't make me hard. My gaze narrows on her lips, and I picture the way they would be wrapped around my dick as I thrust into her mouth. As she takes control over me by sucking me down.

"Pierce?" Charlotte startles me out of my thoughts as I shove a bite in my mouth. I smile at her, trying to rid my brain of the images of her on her knees in front of me.

"Sorry. Just drifted off there."

"How was the shop today? Any new tattoos?" I don't miss what she's doing, trying to steer the conversation away from my earlier question. I'll give it to her, but not for long.

"Good. Nothing overly exciting. Just some walk-ins who wanted butterfly tattoos."

"Do you not like butterfly tattoos?" She sips her wine, her gaze drifting over my exposed ink.

"Eh, not my favourite. I like more challenging pieces." I shrug my shoulder. "Once you've moved on from butter-flies, they aren't the most fun thing to do."

"Would you tattoo a butterfly on me?" Her eyes are dark with lust. Fuck, if I wouldn't love to put my ink on her. I now understand why Sean is so possessive of being the only person to tattoo Ellie.

"Would you want a tattoo?" She slips the fork between

her lips, pulling it out slowly. Damn. The image of her doing that to my cock has me tenting my pants. Again. This woman is driving me crazy in the best way.

"I can't say that I do. Unfortunately, I don't like needles."

"Most people who get tattoos end up not minding needles."

Charlotte gives me a small smile. "I'm pretty sure it's you that helps them through that fear."

"Me?" I don't think anyone has ever said that to me before.

Charlotte pushes her plate away from her and stands, moving to sit on my lap. Her eyes are soft. Big, brown pools that I can get lost in.

"You. You have a way about you that sets people around you at ease. I knew it from the minute I met you. Most people would've been putting on a show for Princess Charlotte, but not you." Her fingers play with the hair at the nape of my neck, and I lean into her touch. The gentle scrape of her nails is electrifying. My entire body is on edge with need for this woman. "I can only imagine how you make the people you tattoo feel. I'm sure if they've never done it before, they must be scared, but you can put them at ease. Make them feel comfortable."

"I don't think anyone has ever described it like that." A shy smile plays on my lips. "Most people would just think I ink people and move on. Nothing like saving lives."

"Don't diminish what you do. Just because you aren't saving lives, doesn't mean you aren't helping people through a hard time with your work. Or helping them move on from a dark time." Charlotte grips my chin, forcing my gaze to hers.

"I like the way you see me." I lean up, claiming her lips with mine. It's a soft kiss. No one has ever looked at my job the way Charlottes has. They see my tattoos and think I'm a bad boy. But that couldn't be further from the truth. And thinking about Charlotte's view has my chest swelling with pride.

"You know, if this whole princess thing doesn't work out, you could be a therapist. You're really good at talking to people." I tuck a loose strand of hair behind her ear.

"Maybe that's what makes me such a good princess," she teases, as I pull her in tighter.

"It also makes you really good at dodging the reason we're here," I whisper into her ear.

She stands, making her way over to the windows. An unease settles over me. "What is it, Charlotte?"

She turns, her arms clutching her stomach. Her eyes hold a sadness that belies the happiness we felt earlier. "I've been told I can't see you anymore."

Shock colours my face. "Can't see me anymore? Says who?"

I stand, crossing the short distance to her. She rears back from my embrace. "The Queen."

"I'm sorry. The Queen says we can't see each other? Why the bloody hell not?" I don't keep the disdain from my voice.

"She seems to think you might be a bad influence on me."

Fuck me. I drag my hand down my face, trying to keep my anger from boiling over. From unleashing it on Charlotte when she isn't the one keeping us from seeing one another. "How am I a bad influence on you?"

I'm pacing around my flat. There's not much room to move, but I keep moving until Charlotte settles a hand on my shoulder. The warmth radiates over me.

"I didn't say I agreed with her." Her voice is soft, but firm. "Why would she get to have a say over my love life?"

"She's the Queen. Kinda seems like she can make you do a lot of things you don't want to do." I step out of the bubble Charlotte's seemed to wrap me in. "I don't know why you had to come all the way over here if you're just going to break things off."

I slump down on the sofa. Fecking hell. I shouldn't be this upset. It was only one date. It's not like we've been dating for years. Just one more person to add to the list of people who think I'm not good enough.

"Pierce. Do you really think I'd come over here to tell you I couldn't see you anymore?" Charlotte's standing in front of me, her arms crossed and her lips turned down in anger.

"Shit. I don't know."

She laces her hands through my hair, tilting my gaze to meet hers. "Do you really think I'd come over here and have dinner with you and kiss you if I was going to break up with you?"

Charlotte straddles me, resting her arse on my thighs. She presses closer into me, as I lock my arms around her waist.

"I don't want to stop seeing you, Pierce." Her breath caresses my cheek.

"You don't?" I hate the need in my voice, but it's there.

She shakes her head. "I don't care what the Queen says, but it does make seeing each other slightly more difficult."

This time, I pull back to meet her gaze. I don't think I've ever heard someone talk about the Queen like this. "It seems like it would be a lot more difficult if we can't be seen together. You live your life in public."

"I do. But it just means we'll have to be careful. Hanging out here together."

"You mean hiding our relationship?" I'm skeptical this

will work. She's a public figure, and the paparazzi are terrible here.

"I don't want to hide you from anyone, Pierce. But if it means that we get to see each other, then I'm all for it."

Her eyes are dancing over my face, trying to get a read on me. I know this will make her life that much more difficult, hiding this. Hiding us. But I've never met anyone like her. Someone that I ache to see after just meeting them. Wanting to hold her in my arms. To hear about all the mundane things she does every day and not get tired of it.

"So sneaking around and staying at my flat because if anyone sees us together…shit, what would happen?" I'm thinking out loud at this point.

"It'd be off to the dungeons for you."

"Think you'd come with me?"

Charlotte leans in for a kiss. Her taste is intoxicating. It's wiping out any annoyance I have at having to keep what we have together a secret.

"You have to admit. We'd probably be the sexiest couple in the dungeons." Her laugh seeps into me, settling me.

I roam my eyes over her face, studying her closely. Her eyes give her away. She's nervous about this. About having to hide or about possibly being caught, I don't know.

"Are you sure you want to do this?" she asks. She's playing with the collar of my shirt, not looking at me.

"Charlotte." My voice is firm. I wait for her to look at me before continuing. "If you're asking if I want to hide away my relationship with you, I don't. I hate that the Queen thinks I'd be a bad influence on you. But if hiding away means we get to be together, then let's do it. I'd stay in my cramped flat for months on end if it means I get to spend time with you."

"I don't know why anyone thinks you'd be the bad

influence." Charlotte kisses me, moving down my jaw. I groan, trying not to rock into her at how good she feels sitting over me. Her hands skate over my arms, tracing the tattoos there.

"You're the bad influence. And I, for one, can't wait for you to corrupt me."

Shoreditch
INK

Chapter Seven

PIERCE

Charlotte's scent lingers over me as I lie on the sofa, staring at the ceiling. My mind is still working on overdrive, replaying the conversation we had. Charlotte wants to keep seeing me, but the Queen is against it. It didn't seem to faze her. But guilt lingers in my gut. Is this something I'm really cut out to do?

When she was here, the decision was easy. That confident smile of hers told me she knew exactly what she was doing. The soft way her lips moved over mine made it easy to forget why continuing on with her is a bad idea.

Our first date was unlike any first date I've ever had. It was perfect. I'd never had more fun in my life. But that's what got us here in the first place.

Except my fingers remember what it felt like to have her luscious curves under them. I wish I could have curled around her all night, feeling her against me. But if she were to be seen leaving my flat, it'd be bad. Very bad.

Christ. Why is this a good idea again?

Charlotte: Hey, handsome. Care to sneak away tomorrow night?

Me: Is that really a good idea?

Charlotte: Where's your sense of adventure?

Me: Just trying to play by your rules

Charlotte: I like a man who knows how to follow instructions

Bloody hell, and now I'm hard. To think, I've seen this woman everywhere for most of her life, and now I'm getting to see this side of her. I shouldn't like her as much as I do, but damn, if she isn't casting a spell on me.

Charlotte: Come on...I want to see you

Me: How can a man turn down an offer like that?

Charlotte: Brill. I'll make it worth your while

Excitement replaces the guilt I'm feeling in my gut at the prospect of seeing Charlotte tomorrow night. Oh, right. This is why I agreed to Charlotte's plan.

We're playing with fire, and it's only a matter of time before we're incinerated.

I FEEL LIKE JAMES BOND. Looking around the pub, I see Charlotte stand from a secluded booth. Her long hair is

tucked away in a hat that hides her face. If you weren't looking closely, you wouldn't know it was her. The dingy pub outside of London wasn't the kind of place I expected Charlotte to know about.

Hell, I didn't even think we could come to someplace like this. When she told us we had to keep our relationship a secret, I assumed it would be a lot of nights hidden away in my flat.

"Wanted to live on the wild side tonight." Her arms wrap around my waist, and she places a kiss on my lips.

"I don't think I've ever heard of this place before." The place is completely empty. Aside from one or two people hunched over the bar, the dark restaurant holds two extra patrons. Us.

Charlotte slides into the booth, and I sit next to her. "How'd you find this place? Doesn't seem very princessly."

"Princessly?" Charlotte eyes me over the pint glass she's sipping on. "I overheard some of the security guys talking about it. They come here after shift and aren't bothered, so I figured it was a good place for us."

"What'll it be?" A gruff voice comes from behind me.

"Another pint and two steak and ale pies." I don't turn to face him as he shuffles off.

"Pretty presumptuous there that I'd like a pie for supper." Charlotte takes another sip, licking the amber liquid from her lips.

The server drops the pint, sloshing it on the table. He doesn't pay any attention to us. It's the perfect spot for us.

"Guess I should've asked. Do you like pie for supper?" I cock an eyebrow at her.

"Anything with gravy, yes. How do you think I get such great curves?"

The beer does little to cool me as my eyes drink her in. The memory of those curves is ingrained in my head after feeling them while playing mini golf. I wrap a hand around her waist, tugging her closer to me. My hand lingers before pulling away.

"You're quite surprising."

"Why do you say that?" Her piercing eyes hit me square in the chest. I should not be feeling this way about her. Not when we've only seen each other a handful of times.

"You say what you're thinking. You don't hold back. I like it."

Charlotte props an elbow on the table, resting her chin in her palm. "You might be one of the only people to say that."

I nod, gulping down my beer. "Because you're a princess?"

She taps a finger to her temple. "Sneaky like James Bond and smart. Quite the package."

"What can I say?" I give her my best smile. "I aim to please."

Charlotte slides closer to me, her breath ghosting my face. "Keep doing what you're doing. You're quite pleasing."

Fecking hell. If I make it through this evening without having to whack one off in the loo, I'll consider it a win. This woman is driving me mad with need.

"Would it please you if I did this?" I slant my mouth over hers. Her deep red lips are soft and pliable under mine. Charlotte deepens the kiss, her tongue sweeping into my mouth.

Everything about this woman is unexpected. I expected someone quiet. More worried about how the media portrays them, like Ellie. But Charlotte is a breath of fresh air.

She takes what she wants. She doesn't hide who she is.

She's a lioness, ready to strike when she finds her prey. I'm just glad it's me.

"Right. Enjoy." Dinner is dropped onto the table without ceremony, as I drag my lips from hers. Charlotte's biting her lip, staring at my mouth.

"To be continued." She pulls her dinner in front of her but stays glued to my side. The heat from her body does nothing to douse the raging inferno burning through me.

"What's your favourite flavour of ice cream?" Charlotte takes a steaming bite of pie, licking her fork clean.

"Random much?" I eye her over my own bite. Long lashes flutter against her cheeks as she swallows her bite.

"Not random. I want to get to know you. Twenty questions style."

"Isn't twenty questions supposed to be yes or no questions?"

She pokes her fork in my direction before taking another bite. "Yes, but I want to get to know you better, and yes or no questions don't cut it."

"But your favourite flavour of ice cream does?" Gravy sits on the corner of Charlotte's mouth. I thumb it off, licking it into my mouth. Even the gravy tastes better with her.

"For all I know, you could be a monster and not like ice cream. What kind of person doesn't eat ice cream?"

"Someone who doesn't eat dairy?"

She rolls her eyes at me. "Fine. But you still haven't answered my question."

"Mint chocolate chip. You?" I take another hearty bite. "Bloody hell. This might be the best pie I've ever had. Don't tell my mum I said that."

"Aww, I won't tell her. You know I have her number now."

My fork clanks down on the plate in front of me. "Of course you do. She has no boundaries."

"It's sweet how much she loves you guys. She does throw quite the party."

"I should say Ellie's mum throws quite the party. Mum was just going to have something at Sean and Ellie's. The Queen made it into so much more."

"And I remember thinking how upset I was I didn't get to talk to the handsome stranger."

A smirk plays on my lips. "Handsome stranger, huh?"

A blush creeps up Charlotte's cheeks. "I might have to take back those words."

"Are you sure? Even if I bring you ice cream?" I finger a lock of her hair, feeling the silkiness.

"Only if it's butterscotch."

My lips snarl on their own. "Butterscotch? That's the worst."

Charlotte shoves me to the side. "And here I thought you were perfect."

"Sorry to shatter any illusions. I should be given sainthood by being seen in public with you considering your terrible taste in sweets."

She leans in, giving me her best smile. "You're pretty sweet. I think that makes up for my abysmal taste in ice cream."

"Damn. And just like that, you're back to being pretty perfect."

"I try." She takes her last bite, the tines of her fork playing on her lips. "Coolest place you've ever travelled? Mine was Norway."

"And here I was expecting someplace more exotic."

Charlotte laughs. "I think I was ten. My granddad went to visit with the king, and he took Ellie, James, and me along. They had kids our age, and we spent the whole time sledding and snowshoeing. It was the most fun I ever remember having."

"Sounds like I'll need to add Norway to my list of places to go."

"I'd love to go back. Traveling is much harder for me now. I have to get clearance to go, so it's much harder to go on holiday for the fun of it."

"So no beach holidays for you then?" The thought of Charlotte lying topless on a private beach somewhere slams into me. Sliding into her tight pussy while I sink my teeth into that lush bottom lip. Damn it. Now I want to whisk Charlotte away to the closest beach. A little hard considering we're not supposed to be seen together.

"How about you?" Her voice pulls me away from my dirty thoughts.

"Dixon, Idaho."

Confusion mars Charlotte's sexy face. "Idaho? Can't say I've ever been there."

I laugh. "I don't suppose you would have. It's where my mum grew up."

"I think having an American mum blows up the whole concept of perfection."

"Hardy har." I tickle her side as she tries to squirm away. I box her in the booth as she throws her hands up in surrender.

"Fine. Tell me about Idaho."

Memories of my childhood flash through my head. "It was perfect. We went every summer to stay with my grandparents. We have cousins that still live there, but it was everything a little boy could have ever wanted."

"Need anything else?" The server comes by, breaking my stare with Charlotte.

"Two more pints, please. Thank you." Charlotte gives him a warm smile before he heads back to the bar.

"What kinds of things did you do?"

"Fished. Hiked. Learned to make a fire. Horseback riding."

"That sounds like the best way to spend the summer."

"Sean and I used to get into so much trouble. My grandparents own a ranch out there, but they used to spend half the summer chasing us around to keep us from doing something stupid."

"Times like that make me wish I had a sibling." Her voice turns wistful.

I wrap an arm around her shoulders as our fresh drinks are delivered. "Did you ever get lonely growing up?"

She takes a long sip, her eyes staying on mine. "A sibling would've made being in the public eye more manageable. Having someone to lean on when times got hard. But I had Ellie. And James to an extent."

I adjust her hat, looking deeper into her eyes. Whenever I'm around her, my body calms. I never thought of myself as an overactive person, but she settles me.

"I always felt like I lived in Sean's shadow growing up. Even then, I wouldn't trade having a brother for anything."

"Did your parents want you to be like him?"

I snort into my glass over the sip I just took. "My dad's a professor. I don't think he thought his kids would turn into tattoo artists if he could've helped it."

"Then why do you feel like you were living in his shadow?"

"Every schoolteacher always compared me to Sean." My voice gets higher, imitating every teacher I've ever had. "'Why aren't you applying yourself like your brother? Why aren't your grades as good as Sean's? Sean was such an excellent student.'" It all bubbles out of me. I'm not one to talk about it, how I feel less than. But with Charlotte, it's easy. I don't feel the need to hide how I really feel.

"I guess that's the one good thing about not having a sibling. No one to be compared to. Although, everyone thought they knew who I was in school. It drove me crazy through primary school, but I learned to deal with it by the time secondary came along."

"Did they tell you your favourite colour was blue?" I say on a laugh.

"Black, actually. I went through a phase where all I wore was black. It was summer holiday, and the paparazzi swarmed us while we were in Scotland, so everyone assumed it was my favourite colour. It's actually purple."

I drop a chaste kiss on her lips. "So if I want to woo you then, purple flowers, not black, would be the way to go?"

"You think I need to be wooed?"

I shrug my shoulders. "Just need to see how much wooing I need to do."

Charlotte's eyes sparkle with mirth. "If this is you not wooing, I don't stand a chance with you."

I want to puff out my chest and beat on it like a caveman. "You best be prepared then. Because I can woo with the best of them. And Charlotte?" Her eyes are heated as they hold my gaze. "I plan to woo the shit out of you, love."

Chapter Eight

CHARLOTTE

The ballroom is crowded tonight. People on top of people, all hidden behind masks. Because of Halloween, Ellie planned a massive fundraising event for Sean's school with a masquerade theme. Masks required. She was wary about my presence drawing more attention to the event with both of us in attendance, but I wanted to come and support her. Even though she's my cousin, she's still one of my best friends. She and Zara are my team. Without them, I don't know where I'd be.

Growing up in the spotlight, it's rare to have someone know exactly what you're going through, so Ellie and I were lucky to have each other. And even though she gave up this life, my need to support her will never go away.

"Charlotte! You look fab!" Ellie appears, as if out of nowhere, beside me. She sweeps her gaze down my emerald-green dress. The material hugs every curve, dipping low in the front with a dangerous slit up the side to my thigh. My hair is twisted up, hiding the knot of the mask.

A gown like this would never be approved by the palace. But this is an unofficial event, and with my annoyance at Aunt Katherine at an all-time high, I wasn't ready to be told no.

"Me? *You* look incredible. I don't think I've ever seen you so happy." I wrap her into a hug, before she pulls me over towards the bar. The black material of her dress clings to her bump. The gold mask does little to hide her bright blue eyes. She's glowing.

"Please, I feel like a whale. This kid is dancing on my bladder, and it's killing me."

Pierce is with Sean by the bar, a drink in hand. My eyes peruse the suit he's wearing—a fitted blue suit, with a light blue pocket square. Pierce is handsome, there's no doubt about that. I could spend the entire night staring at him, and I wouldn't get my fill. What is it about a man in a suit that makes a woman lose her bloody mind?

"Charlotte. Nice to see you." Sean gives me a kiss on the cheek, but my gaze doesn't leave Pierce. His blue eyes spark with desire under his mask. I can feel the heat from here. How I want to be able to kiss him. Stand in his arms and not have anyone tell me it's wrong.

"You remember Pierce?" Ellie asks.

"I do." I extend my hand for him to shake. I never got to tell Ellie about our date before the Queen made it clear I couldn't see him again. She clearly doesn't bother reading the news. Heat snakes up my arm as he takes my small hand in his much larger one.

"Nice to see you again." He drops my hand, letting his fingers ghost over mine. The fine cut of his jaw and the perfect fit of his suit cause heat to build in my core. This man is pure temptation.

"We have to go mingle. Make sure to talk up the school to get as many donations as you can tonight." Ellie loops her arm through Sean's and drags him off. I turn to the bartender and order a glass of champagne.

"You look unbelievably sexy." Pierce's voice is dripping with lust as he stands at my side, his glass hiding his mouth.

"I can say the same about you." I take my drink, the cool liquid helping to calm my overheated body. Just being near Pierce is messing with my head.

"I didn't think you'd be coming tonight." We move to the side, standing close enough to talk, but not close enough to raise any questions.

"I wanted to support Ellie. She's still family, even if she has stepped away from her royal duties."

"I'm glad you came. But fuck, the things I want to do to you in that dress."

Fire licks down my spine at his words. "And what would you do?"

Pierce moves closer, setting his empty glass down beside me. "I'd kiss my way up your leg, and when I get to the top of that slit, I'd tear that dress right off you. Then I'd work my way up the other side. I'd show you pleasure no man has ever given you before."

Bloody hell. I rub my thighs together, trying to quell the building need in my core. I could come just from hearing those words from his lips.

I look around and see someone start to walk over to me. "It was nice to speak with you, Pierce. Hopefully I'll see you later?"

He gives me a questioning look, before seeing why I changed the subject. He turns, backing away from me. "To be continued."

ALL NIGHT. All night I've been filled with an aching need for Pierce. No matter whom I'm talking with, my eyes find Pierce. The searing heat in those blue eyes of his have been driving me crazy. No matter where I go in this ballroom, we find each other, as if we're two magnets destined to connect.

"Thank God I found you." Ellie is at my side.

"Are you okay?" I look over her to make sure nothing is wrong.

"I just need to sit. I'm absolutely knackered. I forgot how tiring these events are, let alone doing it while almost eight months pregnant."

"C'mon then." I loop my arm through hers and drag her off towards benches on the side of the room.

"Do you want me to go find Sean for you?"

She gives me a sweet look. "Could you? I'm ready to head home. Would you mind staying a little longer?"

I drop a kiss on her cheek. "I'll take care of it."

"You're the best, Charlotte."

I give her a bright smile as I push my way onto the crowded dance floor. Drinks have been flowing all night, and the loud music has enticed people onto the dance floor. It's hard to tell who anyone is behind their mask.

A hand on my stomach pulls me back into a hard body. "Where do you think you're going?"

Pierce's gravelly voice washes over me. This simple touch has me itching to turn in his arms. To kiss him.

"Trying to find your brother so he and Ellie can leave."

His breath is hot on my neck. "And do you plan on going home with anyone tonight?"

Goose pimples break out over my skin. "I did see someone I'd like to take home. Not sure if he has any plans."

The masks were perfect for tonight. I'm not Princess Charlotte. We're just two strangers on the dance floor.

"The only plans he has tonight is to make you his."

Lust coils deep in my core. I bite my lip, stifling the moan desperate to break free at his words.

"I'll meet you back at your flat tonight." Desire hangs on every word.

"Wear the dress. I have big plans for you tonight."

Shoreditch

INK

Chapter Nine

PIERCE

The knock on the door has my dick perking up. I've been on edge all night. Being near Charlotte but not being able to touch her is the worst feeling. When I swing the door open, Charlotte stands there in the same dress, no mask.

I waste no time, pulling her into me and dropping my lips to hers. She opens, and our tongues tangle. I could get drunk off the taste of champagne on her lips alone. I'm hungry for her. To feel her bare skin against my lips.

"Fuck. You've been driving me crazy all night." I drop my forehead to hers, breathing in her scent.

"I hated not being with you tonight." Charlotte's fingers trace over my lips. I capture her thumb, swirling my tongue around the pad. Her teeth sink into her lower lip, stifling her moan. She steps closer, her hard nipples brushing my chest.

"You're here now." I back her slowly into my flat, until she hits the back of the sofa. "And tonight, you're mine." I flip her around, bending her over the sofa. I don't want to waste a minute of our precious time together. I hike her dress up, exposing her hips. I pull her thong to the side, running my finger up her slit.

"Have you been wet for me all night?" I dip my finger lower, running it over her clit.

"Yes." Her voice is breathy. "I want you, Pierce."

"Oh yeah?" I kneel down and sit back on my heels, squeezing the sweet globes of her arse together. "Did you imagine how it will feel when I sink my cock into your tight pussy?" I lick down her slit, savouring the taste of her.

She peeks over her shoulder, locking eyes with me, and shakes her head. "No. I imagined how it would feel while I was riding you. To see me bring you to release."

She plays the role of demure princess, but she's anything but. She's fierce. She's powerful. She's commanding. And she can bring any man to his knees. But somehow, I'm the lucky bastard that gets to worship this woman.

My teeth sink down into the globe of her arse before licking the sting away. Charlotte's gasp urges me on as I plunge two fingers into her hot channel. She pushes back, rocking her hips into me. My other hand wraps around her front, rubbing over her clit.

"Just like that." Charlotte's voice is low with need. My cock threatens to break free of my trousers, but there's nothing I can do about it as I focus on stroking her. I want to be inside her but want her orgasm more. "I'm close, Pierce."

Her pussy contracts around my fingers, as I thrust three fingers inside her. I'm dying for her to come on my fingers, but I want her taste on my tongue more. Pulling my fingers out, I lick down her slit, just as her orgasm slams into her.

"Pierce!" Her calling my name almost makes me come in my pants like a wanker. Fuck. Feeling her come on me and tasting her release is the best nectar.

I pull back, steadying her as I stand behind her. She stands, turning to face me, peeling the straps of her dress off. The green silk pools at her feet. Charlotte stands on her tiptoes, taking my lips with hers. Her fingers toy with my hair, scraping along my scalp. I press my erection into her hip as I unhook her bra.

"So, are you ready to ride me?" I step back as Charlotte takes my hand, leading me back to my room. The soft sway of her hips is mesmerizing. Like leading a thirsty man to water. Her naked body is a sight to behold, as if someone created her from my dreams.

She drops her thong and kicks out of her heels as she lies back on the mattress. Her pussy glistens with her release.

"Bloody hell, do you even realize how sexy you are?" I undo the buttons on my shirt slowly, shrugging out of it. I feel her eyes everywhere.

"Do you realize how sexy you are?" She parrots back at me, rubbing her legs together. I grab her ankles, pulling her towards me.

"You don't get another orgasm unless I say so." Her heated gaze roams over me. She wags her finger, beckoning me over her. Charlotte's lips are soft, peppering kisses along my jaw to my ear. I've never been so fucking hard in my life. All I want is to sink into her sweet heat and feel her pulse around me.

"I don't orgasm until you orgasm." She flips us around, straddling my hips. Her fingers trace my tattoos, lighting my skin on fire.

"So you're in charge now?" I thrust my cock up towards her core, as her fingers drift down my chest. Her lips follow. I've never had a woman take control like this before, and it's a huge turn-on.

Her eyes hold mine as she starts to undo my belt

buckle. She drags my trousers and boxers down as my cock springs free. Her smile is downright wicked as she tosses them to the side.

Charlotte moves back up my body, taking my dick in her hand. A low hiss escapes, loving the feel of her nimble fingers wrapped around me. "I've been imagining this all night."

She takes the head of my cock in her warm mouth, and it takes everything I have not to come down her throat right then. Her tongue and fingers are magic as they work together to make me harder and harder. I fist her hair, loving the sight of her swallowing me down.

"Fuck, Charlotte." I try to pull her off me, but she keeps going. Pushing me closer and closer to release. Tears wet the corner of her eyes as I bump the back of her throat. "I can't be coming down your throat the first time we do this."

She pulls off me with a pop. "And what if that's what I want?" She keeps stroking my cock, slick with her saliva.

I reach over to my bedside table, grabbing a condom. "Next time, love. I want you riding me. Just like you said." She quirks her lips up as she grabs the condom.

"You are lucky you're sexy, otherwise I might just hold out on you." Charlotte rolls the condom down my length, giving me a hard squeeze. She rolls her pussy over my dick. It jumps, wanting to get inside her.

"You're driving me crazy, Charlotte." I squeeze her tits together, thumbing her hard nipples. She rocks over me faster. "I need you inside me." I pull her over me, crashing her mouth to mine. I need her lips on mine. I need to feel her everywhere as she slowly sinks down on my cock. My hands squeeze her arse, holding her still. I go over every step of tattooing to keep from blowing my load. Charlotte shifts her hips, starting to move over me.

"You feel amazing." I thrust up into her, meeting her pace. Her nails digging into my chest cause pain to mix with the pleasure. Heat races down my spine as my balls draw up tight, threatening to explode. I try to move her faster, but she slows down, dragging it out.

"Uh, uh, uh. Not yet." She throws her head back, rocking over me. Charlotte is a vision moving over me. Taking me right towards the edge but pulling back.

"You're such a tease." Charlotte peeks down at me, a smile playing on her lips as she starts to play with her clit. I love a woman who knows what she wants. And Charlotte is going for it.

"God damn it. I'm so close." My thrusts are erratic as I try to chase my orgasm. Charlotte is moving faster, the first flutters of her orgasm starting.

"Pierce. Yes! God, yes!" Charlotte pulses around me as I explode into the condom, thrusting up hard.

"Yes. Fuck, yes." My fingers dig into her thighs as we move through our release together. I've never seen a more beautiful sight than Charlotte, eyes half closed with passion and desire as she stays on top of me. I pull her down, chest to chest. Her sweat-slicked skin is flushed from her orgasm. The sweet scent of her perfume hits me and something settles over me. A feeling like coming home—something I don't think I've ever felt before.

No woman has ever made me feel like this. How can this woman I've only known for a short time make me feel so settled? Like I don't have to reach for more. Like everything in my life is okay. That I'm not living in someone's shadow.

"Thinking some deep thoughts there." Charlotte's voice ghosts over my chest. Goose pimples break out over my skin.

"Just thinking how right this feels."

And it does.
Being with Charlotte right now?
Well, it feels bloody well perfect.

Chapter Ten

CHARLOTTE

"Mm, what smells so good in here?" I push my way inside Pierce's flat. Pierce is in his kitchen, plates of food spread out before him. He looks delectable in that tight black tee of his. Ever since the night of the masquerade ball, all I've wanted is to be around him. Any free moment I get, I'm racing across town to his flat.

I want to be wrapped up in his comfort. Locked away from the rest of the world and those keeping us apart. The Queen. The press. Mum, to an extent. If only they could see the man I see. He's the furthest thing from a bad influence.

"Hi, love." He tosses a towel over his shoulder and greets me with a kiss. "I missed you today."

I press up onto my tiptoes, giving him another kiss. Longer. Deeper. "I missed you too."

He wraps an arm around my waist, tucking me into his side. Different plates of food are spread out in front of us. Asian. What smells like curry. Mini tacos. And... "Is that cereal?" I ask.

Pierce's smile is bright. "I figure since we can't go out to all these places, I can bring all the best of London to us."

My heart catches in my chest. One of the things I hate about having to hide our relationship is that we can't be seen together. I want to be able to go to all these places with Pierce, but they're too public. Prime for the Queen to catch us together.

"I love it. Where do I get to start?" I rub my hands together, leaning over and smelling all the different aromas.

"Relax, Charlotte." Pierce hands me a beer. "Plenty of time to enjoy everything I have. Now, sit so I can serve you."

He walks around the bar, pulling out a seat for me. "What did I do to deserve this tonight?" I can't stop beaming with happiness. One of my favourite things is going to all the fun restaurants around the city. With a city this size, there's no shortage of quirky places to try.

"Just because we can't go out, doesn't mean I can't plan a night that isn't boring."

"I'm finding things are anything but boring with you, Pierce."

I sip the cold beer as Pierce places one of the first dishes in front of me. "For your appetizer, ma'am." His face is full of sass, his eyebrows waggling at me. "We have Asian fusion pork belly tacos with a crème sauce. Pairs perfectly with the beer you're drinking."

Laughter bubbles out of me. "Will you accept tips at the end of the night?"

Pierce leans across the counter, capturing my lips with his. "Not in the form of currency, no."

"However will I afford my dinner then?"

Pierce's eyes sparkle with mischief. "I can think of a few ways to pay your server back."

He moves closer, hoping to sneak a kiss. I pull back. "I only pay for exceptional service."

"Better up my game then."

I grab a mini taco off my plate, my gaze locking with Pierce's as I take a small bite. The flavours burst to life on my tongue, and I let out a very unladylike groan.

"I don't think I've ever tasted anything more delicious than this." I shove the rest of it in my mouth. The sweet and spiciness of the Asian flavours are perfect together. "Where is this from? I want to eat only this for the rest of my life."

Pierce's face is lit up with satisfaction. "Circus. I had a feeling you would like them. If you're at the restaurant, there's this whole show they put on." He grabs one and puts the whole thing in his mouth. There's no bitterness in his tone that we have to stay here and can't experience the show together.

"I like that you know what I like," I say over the bite in my mouth. It's not becoming of a princess, but Pierce doesn't care. I can be myself around him. Not have to worry about anyone snapping an unflattering photo to be out in the world for the rest of time.

"Well, I hope you'll like this too." Pierce pushes a small bowl filled with cheese and bread towards me.

"Cheese? This doesn't seem very exciting." I tear off a small piece of bread, still warm, and drag it through the gooey concoction.

"The entire restaurant is cheese. It's all they serve. Who doesn't love cheese?"

The same could be said of Pierce and the adoring eyes he's aiming my way. Who would go to so much trouble to get all this food from restaurants all over the city? It's nights like these, with Pierce, that make all the sneaking around worth it.

"You're looking awfully thoughtful over there, love." Pierce's blue eyes focus on me.

My life isn't easy. People can't handle the press and the rigid standards we have to live by. It's what made Michael leave. Even though we have to hide, being with Pierce is easy. With the way he makes me feel, I'd gladly spend all my days tucked away here if it means I get to be with him.

"Just enjoying the company tonight. I love finding new places and now, I can't wait to go and visit them all." I take another dip of the cheese, but Pierce grabs my wrist, taking his own mouthful. The way his jaw works as he chews is mesmerising.

"Maybe it's something we can do some day." There he goes again. Making plans when I have no idea what our future holds. How long can the two of us sneak around like this? The thought is ice water in my veins. I love being with Pierce like this. Us in our own little bubble. But it can't last, right?

"Try this now." Pierce pushes a steaming, orangey soup towards me.

"What is this?" I inhale. "And why does it smell like peanut butter?"

"Because it is peanut butter. Peanut butter stew from West Africa."

I take a hearty spoonful. Peanut butter. Carrots. Sweet potatoes. "This seems like it would be weird, but wow." I take another bite, tamping down the errant thoughts.

"It's one of my favourites." Pierce has scarfed down half his bowl by the time I look up.

"Where is this from?"

"It's from a small food truck. The owner is from Ghana and came in for a cover-up. Told me all about making the dish from his country. I went the next day and tried it.

Been going every week since. Great mate of mine now. Even plays football with us now. "

I sink back into my chair, finishing off my beer as Pierce sits beside me. "I bet you meet a lot of interesting people."

He nods, sipping on his own drink. "Like you wouldn't believe. But you have to meet a lot of interesting people too."

He pulls my feet into his lap, rubbing the soles. "That is heavenly." His touch soothes away any thoughts on how this won't last. On how this won't work.

"I meet a lot of great people," I say, going back to his question. "But they always put on a front for meeting the princess. The kids are the only ones who don't have any airs about them when they meet me. They're my favourite."

"Do you see yourself having kids?"

I swallow the steaming bite of soup, washing it down with beer. "Two. I've always wanted them. What about you?"

"Never thought about it before. Wasn't with anyone serious. But I could be swayed."

The look in his eyes tells me what, or who, could sway him. "Oh, yeah?"

"Seeing how happy Sean and Ellie's baby makes them, and he or she isn't even here, makes me want that same kind of happiness."

"They are so good together." I take the last bite of soup, not sure what else Pierce has for me.

"Kind of makes you wish we could be together like that?" His voice takes on a melancholy tone.

"What do you mean?"

"That I could hold your hand in public. That I could

kiss you whenever I want to. That you could spend the night here."

I laugh. "Sorry to burst your bubble, but spending the night is frowned upon if you're a royal. Can you imagine the scandal?"

"Princess Charlotte is a hussy! Seen leaving boyfriend's flat in the early morning hours!" Pierce emphasises each word with his hands.

"Oh, so I'm a hussy now?"

Pierce pulls me closer to him. "Only for me. Now do you want the last dish?"

"I don't think I can eat anything else." I lean back in the chair.

"Are you sure? You haven't had dessert yet."

My ears perk up. "Is that the cereal?"

"Thought it'd be fun to try for dessert instead of breakfast." He leans across the counter to grab the colourful bags. I twist my fist into his shirt, pulling him back towards me.

"I can think of something else I'd like for dessert too."

Pierce's eyes darken with need. "Oh yeah? Perhaps a coffee? Tea?"

I smack his shoulder. "I guess you don't want what I'm offering up then. Guess I should just call it an early night."

I drag my feet out of Pierce's lap, feeling how hard he is for me. I stand, moving between his legs. "Guess I'll see you in a few days then?" I whisper in his ear.

Pierce pulls me closer, moving his hands under my jumper and running them along my bare skin. A cunning smile cuts his face.

"I guess dessert can wait."

Chapter Eleven

CHARLOTTE

"Okay, if you could have any job, what would it be?" My fingers trace the intricate tattoos on his chest. The peaks of the mountains that cross his chest.

"What makes you think I'm not doing my dream job?" Pierce is relaxed, his head resting on his arm against the pillows. Soft light filters in from the streetlights outside. His fingers are brushing through the tangles in my hair, no doubt put there by his hand being fisted in it while he was pounding into me.

"Did you always want to be a tattoo artist?" I ask. Pierce captures my hand, bringing it to his lips.

"I actually wanted to move to Australia and become a surfer."

I sit up, and Pierce moves with me. I crawl into his lap, and his leg bends, letting me rest against it. This intimate way we're together? It's relaxing. These quiet moments with Pierce are my favourite. I'm not the princess. We're just two people spending time together. Loving each other's company. No pressure from the outside world. No one telling us we can't be together.

"Can I ask the obvious question?" Laughter laces my voice.

His face lights up. "If I can surf?"

I nod my head, biting my lip to keep my laughter to myself. "Seems like something you would need to know how to do if you wanted to move to Australia and surf."

He shrugs his shoulder. "Mum took us to the beach in Nice when we were little. Dad was giving a lecture at a uni there, so we got to tag along. I remember seeing the surfers and wanting to be just like them."

I lace my fingers with his. "And have you tried surfing?"

"I did once. Total, absolute crap at it. Kind of killed the dream of moving Down Under."

I lean closer to him, my lips a breath from his. "I'm kind of glad you didn't move to Australia."

"Because you wouldn't be here with me right now?"

I nod, dropping a kiss to his lips. "And I'm rather enjoying your company right now."

Pierce's mouth claims mine, his powerful lips moving against mine, his tongue sweeping into my mouth. I lean into his touch, wrapping my arms around him. The easy caress of his tongue starts a fire in my belly. I can't get enough of this man.

He pulls back, his eyes hooded with lust. Will my desire for this man ever be sated?

"What about you, love?" He peppers my face with kisses. "What would you be doing with your life if you weren't a princess?"

"Roller derby girl." My answer comes without hesitation.

"Of all the things in the world, I didn't expect you to say that." Pierce tucks a loose strand of hair behind my ear.

"What, I don't look like I could be a roller derby girl?" I pull back, waving my hands over my body.

"If this is how a roller derby girl looks,"—his warm hands squeeze my breasts together—"then I've been missing out."

Arching into his touch, I try to quell the desire now racing through me. "We went to a roller derby once growing up—I can't remember why—but I remember thinking how badass those women were. I wished I could've been like them." There's a wistfulness in my tone that Pierce doesn't miss. "It's one of the reasons why I want to start this charity for women. To make them all feel like the badass women I know they can be."

"You're pretty incredible, you know that?" Pierce's eyes are soft as he meets my gaze.

"You're just saying that."

"Just because you're not a roller girl, doesn't mean you're not a badass. Your nickname should be Princess Badass."

I bury my laughter in Pierce's neck. "You know just what to say to make a girl feel good."

"Only good?" Pierce wraps me in his arms and flips us on the bed, his weight settling over me. "I must not be doing my job if I don't make you feel like the powerful badass you are every day."

This man. This man takes my breath away. Every other man I've been with made me feel like they were doing me a favour by being with me. I'm self-aware enough to know that my life is hard. That not a lot of people want to take on what the crown requires of them.

But Pierce did it without blinking. Can't be seen in public? *Come to my flat.* Not being seen together at the same event? *No problem.* How can one man be this good?

I run my hands down his spine, his skin pebbling

beneath my fingers letting me know how my touch affects him. "Would you be my cheerleader as I raced around a rink in a short little skirt? Tattoos covering my arms?"

"Tattoos? All this untouched skin you have…just think of the tattoos I could give you…" he trails off.

"What kind of tattoos would you give me?"

Pierce's face is thoughtful. "You'd have a sleeve of flowers. Soft and gentle. But vines of thorns for your badass side." His hand traces down my arm, as if he's imagining the ink there. He rests on his elbow, moving his hand between my breasts.

"And here, you'd have the female symbol." My nipples harden with his hands caressing the underside of my breasts. "Hidden so only I know it's there. Knowing that you're this badass woman who doesn't take shit from anyone, but wants to help everyone around her? Yup, total badass." He traces the pattern on my skin, his fingers lighting a fire inside me.

"What about your face on my arm?"

Pierce shakes his head. "Fuck, no. No names or faces. Shop policy."

My lips turn down in a frown. "So you'll never get your badass roller derby girl tattooed on you?" I trace an empty space on his side. "You don't want me in roller skates and a short skirt right here?"

"Fecking hell." Pierce rolls his hardening erection into me. "Now all I want is to put that bloody tattoo on me and be a cheerleader for you while you knock out other women on skates. You'd be the sexiest one out there."

"And I'd have the sexiest man on my side. All the women would be drooling over you."

Warmth washes over Pierce's handsome face. "I'd have eyes for only you. No other badass could sway me."

Our lips crash together. It's gnashing teeth and tongues

as we fight for control. I love the give and take that Pierce and I have. Some days he takes control, but most of the time, he relinquishes it to me. But now, we're fighting to dominate this kiss. I plant my feet to flip us, but Pierce pushes me down into the bed. His hips grind into me as I tear my mouth away. His lips trail down my neck, hot, searing kisses making me wet with need.

I grab a condom from the nightstand, rolling it down his hard length. He doesn't waste another second before thrusting deep inside of me.

"Pierce," I moan, desire and need evident in my voice. My fingernails dig into his back, urging him on.

"Fuck, Charlotte." He picks up speed, and I already feel my orgasm racing down my spine. His lips drift down my neck, nibbling and sucking. My hands move down his taut back, skirting the top of his arse, pulling him into me on every thrust.

"You." Kiss. "Feel." Kiss. "Amazing." Pierce's words are lighting me up from the inside out.

"Don't stop."

I'm on the edge of the cliff, ready to fall over, when Pierce slows down.

"I'm so close!" My voice is whiny.

"I can't have you coming too quick. What would you think of me if a few pumps and you come?"

I lean up to him, my lips tracing the shell of his ear. "That you're a fantastic lover."

"Damn it, Charlotte. You don't play fair."

I squeeze his arse. "I could say the same of you."

Pierce growls, picking up his pace again. It doesn't take long. I was on the cusp before, but a few thrusts and I'm exploding around him.

"Pierce. Yes!" Pierce surrounds me. His arms. His

scent. Everything about him swirls around me as he starts to come.

He's a sight to behold. The way his neck is tightly corded. How his chest ripples. The flush of his skin. Pierce is the sexiest man ever. And watching him come undone like this prolongs the need that's taking over my body.

Pierce stills inside me. His hair falls into his eyes. Tucking it back, I pull him to me, his lips meeting mine in an easy kiss.

"I wish you didn't have to go."

"I wish I could stay."

We laugh, our words spoken at the same time. No matter how long we're together, it's too short. I want more time with him.

"One day, Charlotte. One day we can be together. Just you and me."

I know it's not that easy, but for just one moment, I picture Pierce and me—holding hands, walking through the park, and attending events together. Just being together.

"Mm, one day." I hug him to me, not ready to let him go just yet.

"One day sounds pretty great."

Chapter Twelve

The loud beat from the club vibrates through me. Even in the VIP section, it's loud. Tiny rooms make up this level of the club. It's one of the only places I knew Pierce and I could get some privacy. I was able to sneak in without anyone seeing me. Drinks, courteous of my security team, were waiting. Now all that's left is for the man of the hour to arrive.

Sipping on my champagne, I glance at my watch. He should be here any minute. We've camped out at his flat these last few weeks, but I could tell we were going stir-crazy, so I suggested a night out at the club. Pierce was hesitant, but I knew we could get away with it. James always was able to when he was here with the women he used to hook up with. But now it's me waiting for Pierce.

As if my thoughts conjured him, Pierce walks through the door, clicking it shut behind him. He is delicious. His mere presence takes over my every nerve as I get my fill of him. Dark jeans. White T-shirt that shows off all his tattoos. I never thought I'd find a man with tattoos so sexy, but Pierce is drool-worthy.

"I was getting antsy." I uncross my legs, setting my drink down as he approaches me. The clean scent that is all Pierce overwhelms me.

"Can't have that, now, can we?" He drops a kiss on my lips before sitting next to me. "Had I known you'd been waiting long, I would've gotten here much faster."

"Couldn't have you seen with me coming in." I hate that we have to hide what we have. Every part of me lights up the moment I see him. The moment I even think about him. I've never been so enraptured by someone before.

Pierce pulls me closer into his side. Not a breath of air is between us. "I get you now, though. That's all that matters." He pushes my hair over my shoulder as his lips find the spot on my neck he loves kissing so much. "Fuck, you are gorgeous." His hands roam over the short, leather miniskirt and silky tank top I'm wearing, one that shows off my curves nicely.

"I've missed you." It's only been a few days since I last saw him, but whenever I leave him, I can't help but feel I might not get to see him again.

"Long day?" He grabs a beer off the tray in front of me and pops it open.

I tuck myself into his side, needing to feel him. To finally relax. "You could say that."

Pierce's long fingers slide under my chin, tilting my gaze to meet his. "What happened?"

"You don't want to hear about my day. People have it way worse than I do." My fingers play with the collar of his shirt and the exposed ink there.

Pierce's eyes don't leave mine as I let out a breath. "On top of the Queen rejecting my proposal again, I was told by several people today how much they miss Eleanor, and how wonderful of a job she did with their organization. I know everyone loved her, but don't they see that I want to be there?"

"Maybe it'll just take some time for them to get to know you. They have to see what a big heart you have."

"I'm tired of everyone thinking I'm the sad, castoff princess." I gulp down the rest of my champagne.

Pierce tucks a loose strand of hair behind my ear, before dropping his hand to my knee. "I don't see you that way."

I pull back, looking into his eyes. "And how do you see me?" My voice is soft, barely heard over the bass pumping through the club.

"I see a strong, confident woman." He drops a hot kiss on my neck. "I see someone who sees what she wants and goes after it." A kiss on my jaw. "I see a woman so full of spirit that nothing will stop her from getting what she wants. Not even the Queen."

Butterflies swarm my stomach. Anytime I'm with Pierce, all the second-guessing goes away. I don't know what it is about him, but he calms me in a way I've never needed before.

My life was good. Even becoming third in line didn't change much. I was happy. But then Pierce came along and showed me exactly what I was missing.

"I wish everyone saw me the way you do." I trail my fingers over his face. This beautiful face that I'm falling for.

The flashing lights overhead change as a new song comes on. Pierce is tapping the beat of the music on my leg. Every beat sends a pulse racing through me.

I pull Pierce up. "Dance with me."

"Your wish is my command, princess." His lips quirk up into a smile. But his eyes belie him. Heat dances behind his darkened irises. Warm hands land on my hips, skating underneath the waistband of my short skirt.

I throw my arms over his shoulders, pulling myself closer to him. "You are the sexiest woman I've ever laid eyes on," he whispers in my ear as his hands drift lower, squeezing my arse as he tugs me to him. His erection is hard against me.

I sway my hips to the music, getting lost in the sensations around me. Of Pierce. Of the alcohol flowing through me. There's nothing but me and Pierce and the music. There're no worries about why I'm not good enough, who will see us, or why we can't be together. Everything fades to the background.

Pierce's lips ghost over my neck as I throw my head back. They drift lower and lower, driving my need for him higher and higher.

Throwing a leg around his hips, I grind into him, needing the friction. I've never felt so wanton in my life. Nothing has ever felt as good as when I'm with Pierce.

He starts to pull the cup of my top down, revealing more of my breast to him. He licks and sucks at the tender skin. I arch into his touch, wanting to tear my top off entirely to be at his mercy.

"Someone's needy tonight." His breath is hot against my overheated skin.

I pull his face to mine. "I need you." His eyes are dark with need, matching my own. Pierce's lips crash down on mine. This kiss is hard. Hot. Needy. I never want it to end. With one hand holding my body to him, his free hand drifts up my thigh.

"You want me like this?" His finger traces over the damp material of my thong, my need for him evident.

I bite down on my lip. I nod in response, my grip on his biceps tightening as he slips a finger inside me. "Bloody hell, have you been like this all night?"

"Whenever I'm around you." My voice leaves me on a

gasp as he starts thrusting his finger in and out of me. The heel of his hand is grinding down on my clit.

My pleasure is ratcheting to new heights. I'm shamelessly riding his hand, wanting nothing more than to find release with Pierce at this moment.

"Do you know how sexy you look right now?" His eyes are locked onto mine. "You're every man's wet dream, and yet somehow you're mine."

I wrap one hand around his neck, bringing him closer to me. "I only want to be yours," I whisper to him. His lips are everywhere on me as he sinks two fingers inside me.

"Yes, just like that, Pierce!" Any decorum of how to carry myself in public is out the window at this moment. It's just me and Pierce as he's driving me closer and closer towards an epic orgasm.

When his lips come down on mine again, my release shatters through me. The noise of the club fades to the background as I hold onto Pierce for dear life. Not a breath of air is between us as he coaxes me through my orgasm.

When I finally come down, he pulls his fingers out and sucks them in his mouth, tasting my release.

"There's nothing like watching you come all over my fingers." His eyes are hooded with lust as he gazes down on me. "I don't know what I did to deserve you, Charlotte."

His voice betrays his eyes. It's laced with a need I feel down to my bones. I don't know where I found Pierce, but I'm not ready to let him go yet. Even if this game we're playing is dangerous.

He sits, pulling me down on top of him. I'm utterly spent. "I should say I'm the lucky one." My fingers brush his cheeks. "Making you sneak around like this. No one should have to do that." My voice drops, even as I try to hide the anguish that laces it.

Pierce lifts my chin, forcing my focus on him. "You are

worth it, Charlotte. Don't ever doubt that you are. I'd spend years sneaking around if it meant I got to have you. In any way."

There aren't enough words to express what his mean to me, so I pull his lips to mine. It's a sweet kiss. Easy, languid strokes of my tongue meeting his.

"You're too good to me, Pierce."

"You make it easy, love." He reaches forward, passing me my drink before grabbing his. The cool liquid is refreshing to my overheated body. We stay like this, in comfortable silence as the music and lights continue to pulse around us.

"Do you need to be home soon?" he asks. My fingers skate over the tattoos on his arms.

I shake my head. "Not Cinderella tonight. No events tomorrow, so I can stay here with you as long as I like."

"Fecking hell, if that isn't an invitation." His heated words are a fire licking my skin.

I nip at his earlobe. "I'd close the club down if it meant I got to be here with you all night, but you know we can't."

His breath escapes him on a sigh. "Just means we have to make the most of the time we do have."

"I like the sound of that."

His lips capture mine in the sweetest of kisses. Everything about this man should scream bad boy, with the tattoos and intense eyes that hide his emotions. But not to me. He reveals everything to me with one glance. I love that he doesn't hide from me. Most men wouldn't show their true colours to a princess. But not Pierce.

He lays everything out for me. I could never get enough of this man. His touch. I shouldn't want him as much as I do, but I can't help it. His touch has brought me back to life.

He grabs my chin, changing the angle. Deepening the kiss. I straddle his lap, grinding myself over his erection.

"If you keep doing that, I'm going to come like a teenager in my pants."

I pull back, giving him a naughty grin. "Then we can't have that, can we?"

Finding the zipper, I pull it down. Reaching into his pants, I find his hard cock leaking.

"Fuck, that feels amazing," he says on a hiss. Wrapping my hand around his hard length, I start stroking as he tips his head back in pleasure. He rocks into me as I pump, moving my hand up and down. I slide off his lap, kneeling before him. His eyes are hungry as I take the tip of his hard cock into my mouth.

Pierce's hips buck off the bench, as I take him deeper. I push up his shirt, trailing my fingers over the lines in his abs. His hands fist through my hair, guiding my motions.

My eyes lock on his, not pulling away. I move my hand down, gripping the base and working him in tandem with my mouth. The hard floor is biting into my knees, but I don't care.

I've never done anything like this. Never felt so dangerous before. I hollow my cheeks and take as much of Pierce into my mouth as I can. My eyes water as I suck him down.

"Fuck, I'm going to come." His voice is gravelly. Pierce tries to pull me off of him, but I swat his hand away as the first spurts of cum hit my tongue. I drink it down. I take every last drop of his orgasm before I pull off him. His eyes are closed, his chest heaving with his quick breaths.

I wipe the corners of my mouth before I settle next to him. "Damn, Charlotte." He tilts his head to the side, opening one eye to look at me. "That was...wow."

I pull him in for a kiss, not wanting to lose the connection with him. It's getting late, and I know we'll have to leave soon. Each time, it gets harder and harder to leave him.

"I have to say, tonight was a pretty good night." I drop my forehead against his. A small smile plays on the corner of Pierce's lips.

"We should definitely come here more often."

Chapter Thirteen

CHARLOTTE

"You seem really happy." Zara stretches up in a warrior pose. We've been getting together to do yoga on Saturday mornings as often as our schedules allow.

"It's just been a good few weeks." *And an even better night at the club.* I try to hide my grin, going into downward dog.

"The last time I saw you, you were moping about. What changed?"

It might have to do with a certain handsome man, but I can't tell her that. I hate that I have to keep my relationship with Pierce a secret from Zara. Seeing how happy Zara and James are, as well as Ellie and Sean, makes my heart ache that I can't shout about my relationship.

"Just reframing how I'm going about things. No sense in moping, as you say, when things won't change."

Zara drops her pose, sitting on the yoga mat in her study. "Just like that?"

I peer between my arms, her body upside down from my angle. "Just like that."

"And here I was worried about you."

I drop my knees to the ground, sitting back on my heels. "Why were you worried about me?"

A sheepish look washes over Zara's face. "You just seemed so unhappy. I know you went out on a date with Pierce and had a great time, but nothing came of it."

I try to school my features, but I can't keep the smile from spreading.

"Nothing came of it, right?" I hesitate, only for a moment, before Zara's eyes widen. "Are you still seeing him?"

I shush her, waving my hands in front of her. "Of course I'm not still seeing him."

"Then why are you blushing?"

I pat my hands over my cheeks, trying to quell the growing heat in my face. "It's warm in here."

"Bollocks. It's a drafty old palace, and it's barely five degrees outside. You're sleeping with him, aren't you?" Zara's voice echoes throughout the room.

"Shut it!" I slap my hand over her mouth, but her eyes are alight in amusement.

"Why are you keeping this a secret from me?" She pulls my hand off her mouth.

"We need drinks for this."

"SO LET me get this straight. You and Pierce had, and I quote, 'the most magical evening of your life,' and the Queen told you you couldn't see him anymore?"

I nod my head, sipping on champagne. It's still early, so we could justify mimosas this morning. "That's basically it."

"All because she's worried that Pierce will take you away from the crown?"

"Yup." I pop the p. "Apparently I don't know how to make my own decisions and could easily be swayed by a man."

"So just like that, the Queen says no, and you hide your relationship?"

"It's either that or give up the crown."

"I just can't wrap my head around it. Why would she think you'd give up the crown?"

"Ellie met Sean and then gave up her place in line."

"But she never wanted to be the Queen in the first place!" Zara shrieks.

"Shh! Keep your voice down." Why couldn't I have just said I was happy because I was working on my own charity? "She hated royal life, but Aunt Katherine only sees what she wants to see. And Pierce is a threat."

"Have you tried talking to her about it?" Zara tries to reason with me, but it won't help.

"No. I can't bear the thought of having to tell her why I want to date Pierce and have her shut me down again." Pain settles in my chest. How could anyone dislike Pierce? With his easy smile that lights up his face, the way he listens to me, and the caring way he holds me. I've never felt with anyone else the way I feel with Pierce.

"I hate this for you." Zara's face is full of sympathy, and I get it, because I hate it too.

"I've only ever had one real boyfriend, and he wasn't cut out for this life." I drain the rest of my mimosa and pour another. This conversation took a heavy turn for a Saturday morning.

"Michael?"

I lick my lips, nodding my head. "I thought he was the one, you know? Granddad loved him, and my parents loved him. Turns out he didn't love me enough to put up with the circus surrounding my life." Tears wet my eyes. Thinking about him now pushes my relationship with Pierce into a harsh light.

"I hate to ask the tough question,"—Zara pauses, squeezing my hand—"but what makes you think Pierce is the one?"

I try to swallow over the nerves bubbling up. "Maybe he's not the one." My words feel forced and fake, but I play it off. "We could decide tomorrow we have no chemistry and want to end things right now."

Zara slaps her hands down on the counter. "Now I don't believe that for a second."

"And why not?"

"Because when you talk about him, you look the same way I do when I think about James. You have love in your eyes."

Covering my eyes with my hands, I rest my head on the counter. "It can't be love. We can't even be together."

The ache in my chest starts to grow. What if Pierce wakes up tomorrow and decides this isn't worth it? That I'm not worth sneaking around for? I don't know if I would survive it.

"And what are you ladies discussing this morning?" James startles me as he makes his way into the kitchen, dropping a kiss on Zara's cheek. Her face warms over at the mere sight of my cousin. I wouldn't be surprised to see hearts coming out of her eyes. These two are so bloody in love, it kills me. Is that the same face that Zara was just talking about?

"Just discussing wedding plans."

"And it's driving you to drink this early?" James quirks a brow at us.

"You've met the royal wedding planner," Zara deadpans.

"Drink away." James leaves just as quickly as he came.

"I love that man, but any time the wedding is brought up, he fakes an emergency just to try and leave."

"Can't trust men with anything." I force a laugh.

"Charlotte, I love you like the sister I never had, so I'm going to give you some tough love."

My heart sinks at her words. Please don't let her tell me to stop seeing Pierce. I don't know what our future holds, but I'm not ready to give him up yet. I'm too selfish for that.

"You need to make a decision, one way or the other. I know you care about him. It's easy to see. But you're doing a disservice to you and to him."

"There's no easy choice here, Zara." I pick at the hem of my workout top, not wanting to feel the full force of Zara's words. It's too hard.

"No one said love was easy."

Chapter Fourteen

CHARLOTTE

"Aren't you just precious?" A woman with hair as white as a cloud pinches my cheek. It's one of the many reasons I love coming to retirement centres. I love the elderly. "We loved your grandfather. May he rest in peace."

"Thank you for your kind words, Edith." She beams up at me from her seat in the community centre. "We loved him dearly."

"Didn't hurt that he was easy on the eyes." Her friend smacks her on the shoulder.

"Don't mind her. She's been on the hunt for a new man since she got here."

I have to hide my laughter. "You would've had to fight Grandmum off for him. She's quite the feisty one."

"Oh, I think I could take her."

"I'd pay good money to see you try," her friend says on a laugh.

"Ladies, we need to show Princess Charlotte a few more areas." The director of the community, Martha, looks mortified at these two women's words.

"I had such fun chatting with you two. It's people like you that make my work so enjoyable." I drop kisses on both of their cheeks.

Edith beams with pride. "Thank you for making these old loons' day." She motions between her and her friend. "My family won't believe I met you."

"Oh, we snapped a few pictures," the photographer in the back pipes up.

"One more?" I step behind Edith, and he gets another photo. "Hopefully your family will believe you now."

After another pinch to the cheek, I'm led into another part of the building. "Thank you for humouring some of our more lively residents. At this age, they tend not to have much of a filter."

"It's quite alright, Martha. My grandmum is the same way. Some of the things she says…" I laugh. Grandmum always has an inappropriate story to tell. Ever since Granddad died, it's like she lost the filter. She no longer makes public appearances, so it's as if she doesn't care.

"She's quite the woman. We all miss your grandfather dearly. But Queen Katherine is doing a marvellous job."

"That she is. She had big shoes to fill, but the Queen is doing a great job."

"Do you know I met your grandfather once?"

I shake my head. "When did you meet him?"

Martha is an easy woman to talk to. With soft features, she has the perfect temperament to run a place like this. "There was an event at the palace to thank healthcare workers. I didn't think I'd get invited, but I was. Both he and your grandmother were quite welcoming. Must say, it was such a highlight to meet him. He had quite the personality."

I smile. "My grandparents were quite the couple. We

were lucky to grow up with them. Seeing them on tours of the world was always special."

"Do you remember when they went to Canada? You might have been too young."

I laugh. "I grew up watching highlights from that tour. They were at a children's hospital, and one of the kids wanted to have a wheelchair race with him. I don't think I've ever seen him so happy."

"It was truly brilliant. It's what made me want to go into this business. Seeing how kind and caring he was made a difference in my life. My mum and I were lucky to have good people in our life. Turned our lives around."

"Turned your lives around?" I give her a questioning look, hoping she'll enlighten me.

"Dad wasn't around growing up. It was just me and Mum. If it wasn't for some friends of hers, we would've been out on the streets. Thankfully, a few of them took us in and gave us what we needed to get started again."

A lightbulb goes off. It feels like a lifting of the fog. This is exactly what I've been waiting for. I pull Martha in for a hug. "Thank you for telling me that. Stories like that are why I love my work. I only hope I can inspire someone like that in the future."

Martha gives me a warm smile. "I can assure you, you are inspiring to a lot of people."

A blush creeps up my neck. I love my work, but I never hear these words enough. And now, with her story, I hope I can inspire and help even more people. "Thank you. I can only hope I will live up to the legacy that my grandparents leave behind."

Seeing how in love my grandparents were makes me yearn for that kind of love. It makes me think I might have found that kind of love with Pierce. It's only been a few weeks, but whenever we're together, I'm happy. Even though we stay in the safety of his flat, we're in our own bubble. But can we exist outside of our bubble?

Only time will tell.

Shoreditch

INK

Chapter Fifteen

PIERCE

The door to my flat swings open, and Charlotte stands there, looking as sexy as ever. She's bundled up tight in a winter coat. It's colder than it should be in November. But the pink on her cheeks and the cute hat she's wearing have me clutching her tightly to me.

"Hi, love. Good day?"

She shivers, her body shaking in my arms. "Fantastic. I've finally realised what I'm going to do for my charity." Her hands snake under my shirt, a cold contrast to my warm body.

"Bloody hell. Let me make you some tea to warm you up, and you can tell me all about it."

The lights from the street flicker into my apartment. It's dark out already. I love the early nights at the shop during the winter months. It means I get more nights like this with Charlotte.

"It's so simple in its brilliance, I don't know why I didn't think of it before."

Charlotte is bubbling with excitement. I don't think I've

ever seen her this happy. The kettle starts to hiss, as I make us each a cuppa.

"Tell me about it."

Charlotte drags me over to the sofa, settling next to me. "I met this incredible woman today, Martha, and she told me her story. How seeing my grandfather racing in a wheelchair with a kid made her want to go into the health-care industry and help people. And how her mum struggled when Martha was growing up."

I listen, not wanting to interrupt her. She sips at her tea, setting it down before grabbing my hands. "I want to help women who are down on their luck like Martha and her mum. If they might not have a place to go, create shelters for them. If they need a hand up in getting jobs, help them that way. Organise job fairs at these different shelters as a way to lift them up."

"And you think the Queen would approve?" I know how much she's been pushing back on Charlotte and not wanting her to do it.

"It's a much narrower scope than what I originally had planned. I really think this could be it, Pierce."

Her eyes are searching mine, as if she needs my approval. I cup her cheeks, still cold. "I think it is absolutely brilliant." I drop a tender kiss on her lips. "I'm so happy you finally found the spark. It's perfect. I don't know how the Queen wouldn't greenlight this for you."

"Really?"

I nod my head. "I want to help. I don't know how I can, but you're the perfect person to do this."

Charlotte drapes her legs over mine, scooting closer to me. "I feel really good about this. Like I was told no before because I was just waiting for this idea."

I love her passion about her job. It shines through in how she talks about her day. She was born to do this work.

"Anyway, enough about me. How was your day?"

I pull Charlotte closer to me. She never wants to keep the spotlight on her. It's one of the things that makes her so wonderful.

"New cover-up piece today. Going to take a few sessions, but it's going to be great."

Charlotte sets her tea down, straddling my legs. "I'd love to see your work someday."

I lift my sleeve up, showing her the ink on my forearm. "I designed all of these myself."

Her fingers trace the ink. The soft touch lights me up. I want to bottle it up and never lose it.

We're quiet, soaking each other in. Her eyes follow her fingers on my skin. It's moments like this that make me think this could work. That Charlotte could have an amazing day at her charity and come home to me. That we could be together for real.

"I've got a question for you." Charlotte pulls me from my thoughts.

"Hit me." My hands run up her thighs. I love that she always wants to sit on me like this, her straddling my lap. The constant need for contact with this one is high.

"What's your favourite sexual position? Or one you've always wanted to try?" Her voice is heavy, desire hanging on to every word.

My cock thickens behind my jeans, pressing into the zipper. "Bloody hell. That's quite the subject change."

Her fingers trace the throbbing veins on my neck. It takes every ounce of strength I have not to throw her down on this couch and ride her until she screams my name.

"I had a conversation with Zara—"

"You were discussing me with Zara?" Panic undercuts any other emotion I'm feeling.

Charlotte looks sheepish, dropping her gaze to her

hands that are now playing with the collar of my shirt. "I couldn't hide it. She's one of my closest friends, and it just sort of came out."

"What if she tells someone?" I'm not ready for this to be over. Sure, I wasn't sure if I could do this at first, but it was a pretty easy decision. Charlotte makes it easy, and I'm not ready to give her up.

"She won't. I'd trust Zara with my life," Charlotte says, her tone forceful, leaving no room for argument.

"I trust you." And I do. It's easy to trust Charlotte, but there's still a niggle of worry that this could bite us in the arse.

"I wasn't discussing you specifically with Zara. She was telling me about this game her friend Marnie got her for their wedding night."

"A game? What kind of game?" My interested is piqued.

"You draw a card, and whatever position you get, that's how you're having sex."

Fucking hell. "And where do we get a copy of this game?" My cock is hard against Charlotte's heated core. There are far too many layers of clothing between us.

"I couldn't possibly go out and buy the game. But I thought it'd be fun to try the ones we want to try tonight." Charlotte's eyes are dark. Darker than I've ever seen them.

"Well then." I kiss her neck, sucking on the tender skin over her throbbing pulse. She tilts her head, giving me better access. "I say ladies first then."

Charlotte runs her hands down my chest. "I want you to tie me up."

"What are we talking about here? Arms? Legs?"

"Just my arms. I've never done it before, and I only trust you to do it."

My lips curl up into a smile. "I think I'm really going to like this game."

I pick Charlotte up, her legs wrapping around my waist. Her mouth moves over my neck as I take us into the bedroom. I drop her in the middle of my bed, watching as her gorgeous tits bounce under her T-shirt.

"I think mine will line up nicely with yours." Dragging a finger along the V of her shirt, I pull it away from her skin, getting a peek of the swell of her breasts.

"And what is yours?"

"I want to fuck these tits of yours." My voice is gravelly, my dick threatening to explode with the tension buzzing in the room. "You have the most beautiful breasts I've ever seen, and I want to see my cock sliding through them. Feel them surrounding me. Come all over your beautiful tits."

Charlotte gets up on her knees, crawling towards me. Her fingers hook into the waistband of my jeans, pulling me closer. The brush of her fingers on my warm skin has me ready to strip her naked and take her right here.

"Then let's get started." The clink of my belt echoes around the room. She pulls it out before moving to pop open the button of my jeans. Her fingers move the zipper down, the snick the only sound I hear. My boxers are tented, the need in me evident as Charlotte palms the bulge.

"Fuck. If you keep doing that, this little game is going to be over well before it starts."

Grabbing the back of my shirt, I pull it over my head and drop it on the floor. Charlotte's eyes track my movement. My skin heats under her stare. I love the way she looks at me. It's how I look at her. Like she's the best thing to ever happen to me.

Charlotte takes her shirt off. Her nipples are diamond hard through the lace cups of her bra. "I can't believe I get to fuck these." I squeeze them together, feeling their heavy weight in my hands. As my thumbs graze her tight nipples, Charlotte arches into my touch.

"What are you waiting for? Tie me up and get to it."

"Patience is a virtue." Hand landing in the centre of Charlotte's chest, I push her back on the bed. She lifts her back up to take off her bra as I take my belt in hand.

"I'll make these loose, in case you want to stop." I lean over her, bringing her arms up with one hand.

"I trust you." Her eyes lock on mine. There's no hesitation in them. I don't take this trust lightly. I claim her lips with mine. The need I have for this woman is undeniable. I thought we'd have a few fun dates and then call it quits because it was too hard.

But the only hard thing is how fast I've fallen for her. I've never had this connection with anyone else. Asking silly questions. And fun questions. Fuck, questions about what sexual positions we want to try. Only a deep sense of trust between two people would move a relationship like this along.

I link the belt around Charlotte's wrists, binding them together through the slats of my bed. "Feel okay?" She tests the strength.

"Perfect."

With a leg on each side of her waist, I gaze at the beauty beneath me. Long dark hair fanned out on my pillow. Lips a deep red. Eyes shining bright with trust.

Standing, I shuck off my pants and boxers, my cock hitting me in the stomach. I grab a condom and lube from the nightstand and go back to Charlotte, continuing my perusal of her body.

"You still have on far too many clothes." I run a single finger down her stomach. Goose pimples break out over her soft skin.

"Whatever shall you do about it?" Her voice is filled with lust. I undo the button and zipper on her pants, pulling them down her legs, a scrap of black fabric covering the pussy that I love so much.

"I think I'm going to fuck this pussy nice and hard. But right before I come, I'm going to fuck these tits." My hands go to them, pinching and rolling the dark nipples between my fingers. "I'm going to come all over your chest." My vision blurs with need. "Fuck. I'm going to claim them as mine. No one else gets these tits but me."

A possessiveness I've never felt settles over me. I've never said anything like that to another woman. But I know I want Charlotte for as long as she'll have me. I want to make her mine in every sense of the word.

Charlotte's legs are rubbing together, and I command, "I don't think so. Your orgasm is mine tonight." I pull her legs apart. Running a finger under her thong, I rip the material away from her body. Her pussy glistens with need.

"Pierce. I need you," Charlotte moans. Gazing up at her, I see she's pulling at her binds.

"Oh, you do?" I sit back on my heels, my gaze roaming over her naked body.

I've had my fair share of sexual experiences, but seeing Charlotte tied up like this is a new one. "Fucking hell, you're absolutely gorgeous."

Charlotte's eyes open, locking onto mine. The world stills around us. It's just the two of us in my bed. Charlotte's not a princess, and I'm not someone she has to hide away from the world. It's just us. Pierce and Charlotte. Charlotte, giving herself over to me in a way I never would have imagined.

Settling over her, I claim her lips. I need the connection. To be as close as possible to her. I kiss down her jaw.

Nibble on her ear. Suck on the elegant slope of her neck. Charlotte pulls against my belt.

"Doing alright, love?" I nibble on her collarbone.

"Ugh. I just want to touch you." I pepper kisses down her chest, lavishing attention on the swell of her breasts.

"I have to say, I like this. Getting to take my time and explore every inch of your body." I squeeze her tits together, flicking her nipples with my thumbs. Her leg is moving under my hard cock, and I have no doubt precum is leaking all over her leg.

"I might have to rethink this next time."

"If you're ready to stop, I have no problem doing so." I pull back, my hands resting on the curves of her hips.

Charlotte gives me a look that would bring me to my knees if I wasn't on the bed already. "If you stop, there will be hell to pay."

The corner of my mouth quirks up. "Your wish is my command then."

Kisses rain down over her stomach, sucking on every inch of creamy skin before nibbling on her hip bone. The smell of her need has me moving faster. Wanting to sink my cock into her tight pussy. To fuck her within an inch of orgasm and then take what I want.

Spreading her folds, I take my time, licking and sucking on her pussy. Swirling the wetness on her clit. Her moans and sighs are making it hard to go slow, but I love making her crazy.

"Are you going to fuck me yet?" I peer up at her, not moving my tongue from heaven. She tastes like the most forbidden fruit. Sinful and sweet, which is my Charlotte in a nutshell.

Sitting back on my feet, I grab the condom and roll it over my hard length. "Are you ready for this? I won't go easy."

I give myself a hard stroke, not wanting to blow my load before I'm between her tits. "I want it hard, Pierce. Fuck me hard."

I sink into her tight pussy. "Fuck. Fuck fuck fuck."

I don't know what it is about tonight, but Charlotte has never felt so good squeezing my cock. Setting an unrelenting pace, I drive into her. My thrusts are quick and hard. Grabbing the lube, I pop the lid open and coat her tits. While I'm playing with her nipples, her pussy flutters around me.

"You like that?"

"God, yes!" Charlotte's eyes are closed, head thrown back in pleasure. Seeing her like this, laid out before me, has my balls coiling up tight.

I pull out of her, taking the condom off. Moving up her flushed body, I take her tits in my hands, squeezing them together as my cock slides through the slickness. The tip bumps her chin.

"Fuck. This is hottest thing I've ever done." I play with the hard peaks of her nipples as I thrust between them, this time long and slow.

Charlotte's eyes connect with mine, and I couldn't look away if I tried. They're dark with need, but the trust there? It's like nothing I've ever experienced. The trust she has in me to do this, to give me control, is something I don't take lightly. The connection is strong. The desire swirling between us causes me to pick up the pace. I want to paint her with my release. To mark her as mine.

I've never felt so possessive of a woman. But Charlotte brings it out in me. She makes me feel things I've never felt before.

The soft moans from Charlotte and her own orgasm shuddering through her body pulls mine from me. Long spurts of cum land on her chest, rolling down her neck and chin. Fuck, if this isn't the sexiest thing ever. I pull back, her breasts thoroughly ravaged. Charlotte's body is soft, sinking into the mattress.

Climbing off her, I undo the belt, pulling her arms down. "I don't think I'll be able to move." Massaging the stiffness in her shoulders, I kiss my way down her arms, paying special attention to the red marks on her wrists.

"You okay?" I grab my shirt from the floor, cleaning her up. Charlotte snuggles into my side as she burrows under the covers.

"I feel amazing." Her fingers dance across my chest as we lie together. It's the perfect moment, soft and tender after what we just did. But it can't last. "I wish I could stay the night."

"I know." I kiss the top of her hand, brushing my hands over the silky locks of her hair. "Maybe just stay a little while longer?"

"Mmm. Okay." Charlotte's voice is soft as she starts to drift off.

This right here is everything. Exactly what I want in life. To have Charlotte by my side in every meaningful way. To protect her from the world but support her however she needs.

The woman I didn't know a few short weeks ago has now become everything to me.

Now, how do I keep everything from slipping through my fingers?

Shoreditch

INK

Chapter Sixteen

PIERCE

"You do realise Thanksgiving is usually celebrated on a Thursday, right?" Peering over Ellie's shoulder, I watch as she continues making dinner with Mum.

"Yes, thank you. But this was the only time your parents could make it, and I wanted to do it before the baby comes, so hush." She shoos me out of the kitchen, but not before I grab another beer.

"Pierce. Have I taught you nothing? Stay out of the kitchen while your mum is cooking." Dad shakes his head at me as I sit beside him in the living room. Ellie told Mum she wanted to learn how to cook a proper Thanksgiving meal, and that none of our input was needed. With an American mum, we grew up celebrating because it's her favourite holiday.

"I wasn't commenting on her cooking skills. I'm not that dumb." I take a long pull on my beer as Charlotte bursts through the front door. Charlotte's coming today? I don't know if I'm prepared to be in the same room as her and not want to touch her.

"I'm not late, am I?" Her cheeks are pink as she shrugs

out of her heavy coat. Christ, does she look beautiful in leggings that hug every curve and a cream sweater that hangs off one shoulder. Her lips are painted a bright red. It takes everything I have not to sweep her up into my arms and kiss that lipstick right off her.

"I'm so happy you could make it!" Ellie comes out of the kitchen, wrapping her arms around Charlotte as best she can. "Better than the rest of the family who couldn't make it."

"I don't think I've ever been to a Thanksgiving dinner before. Anything I can help with?" She gives me a shy look, before following Ellie into the kitchen.

"Are you listening to me?" Sean is giving me a strange look.

"Sorry, what were you saying?" I take another sip of my beer, trying to cool down. Anytime Charlotte is near, I can feel the heat coursing through me. I love what she does to me, but I hate that we have to act like we hardly know each other.

"Did you finish that piece you were working on yesterday?"

I nod my head. "Yup. Definitely not my favourite, but it's what they wanted."

"What'd they want?" Dad asks, attention still focused on the TV.

"It was a bear attacking a lion. Why people want what they want is beyond me," I say, shaking my head. "It was to cover up an old quote on their back."

"I'm sure it was the best bear attacking a lion out there." God love our dad. He's brilliant but doesn't always understand what we do.

"Dinner's ready!" Ellie calls from the kitchen.

The table is set for a feast. Turkey, potatoes of all kinds, rolls, corn. You name it, Ellie cooked it.

"Is Thanksgiving dinner always this much of a to-do?" Charlotte asks, carrying the turkey out.

"In our family it is," Mum answers. "It was my favourite holiday growing up, so I made sure to continue the tradition with our kids."

"Pretty sure we were the only kids in our school who got a random Thursday off school to have dinner," I snicker.

"And yet, you never seemed to mind as a kid." Mum goes to her seat, as the rest of us take any open spot available. The only seat left is right beside Charlotte.

"So, your first Thanksgiving, huh?" I whisper to her.

"Ellie was very excited to make it, so I figured I'd come. Plus," she leans closer, lowering her voice, "good excuse to see you."

Bloody hell. I'm in way deeper than I should be with this woman. Not a soul in this room knows we're dating, and I hate it. I hate that Charlotte's life is controlled to the point where we can't be together. I want to be able to hold her hand and kiss her in front of my family. But we can't.

Because I can't kiss her like I want, I press my leg to hers, wanting the contact. Needing the heat from her to calm my raging storm of emotions.

"Before we tuck in, I'd just like to thank Ellie for making such an amazing meal for all of us. We're so pleased to have you in the family, and I can't wait to meet my future grandbaby." Mum's face is lit up with excitement.

"Cheers!" Everyone holds up their drinks in Ellie's direction.

"I'm so happy you all could make it. I love getting to be with all of you today, even if it's not really the holiday today." She takes Sean's hand as everyone starts to serve themselves.

"Pierce, when are you going to start giving me grand-babies?" Mum asks from her end of the table.

Oh, for fuck's sake. Charlotte coughs into her napkin beside me. "That's a bit of a ways off, Mum. Do we really need to have this conversation at the dinner table?"

She holds her hands up in defence. "Sean is giving me grandchildren. They'll want cousins to play with."

"He'd need to be dating someone before that can happen, Mum." Sean smirks at me from his end of the table.

"Thanks, bro. Appreciate that." I shake my head, hating where this line of questioning is going.

"Is there anyone you can set him up with, Ellie?" Mum asks.

"Christ, can we not have this conversation?" I really don't want to be talking about anyone setting me up when the woman I'm currently dating is sitting next to me.

"Maybe Ruby knows someone at school that would be good for Pierce." Ellie completely ignores me.

I lean back in my chair as Charlotte quietly eats her dinner without looking at anyone. I grab her knee beneath the table, giving it a squeeze. She pulls her leg from mine, uncomfortable with the conversation.

"I'm sure she knows lots of people. Maybe you can find someone for Charlotte while you're at it."

"Okay, Jacqueline. Enough of that. The kids don't need to be set up by their mum." Dad pats her arm, ending the topic. Thank fuck.

An ache settles in my chest. I can feel Charlotte pulling away from me even when we're sitting right next to each other. This fucking sucks. I've finally met someone I truly care about, and we can't be together. It isn't fair, but I'll take whatever Charlotte can give me.

And right now, she's not giving me much.

"Sorry. Just want all of my children to be as happy as we are." She gives Dad a sappy face before kissing him.

"Ugh, we're trying to eat," Sean groans, covering his face.

"Oh, like you two aren't going to kiss in front of your kid all the time. I know what you do in the office." I wave my fork between the two of them, before popping another bit of turkey in my mouth. Christ, that really is good.

"And what is it that you two are doing in the office?" Mum shifts her focus to Sean, thank God.

"Not cool, bro." He shakes his head. Ellie's face is redder than a tomato.

"You okay?" I whisper to Charlotte, the attention all on Sean and Ellie.

"Fine." Her voice is sharp, and she won't even look at me. She's anything but fine. Fine is the most dangerous word in the English language.

"Can we talk later? Maybe head over to my place after?"

"I'm tired. Maybe another night. I've got a busy day tomorrow, so maybe later this week." Fecking hell, Mum had to go and open her mouth, and now Charlotte can barely look at me.

"If that's what you want."

Charlotte

"MISS CHARLOTTE. Are you going to find a prince?"

Oh, bloody hell. Ever since Thanksgiving dinner this

past weekend, it seems everyone has an opinion on my love life.

"Maybe one day, darling. But not today," I answer the small child. I've spent my morning at a new children's hospital outside of London. Normally I love this, but a rain cloud has been following me around since Sunday.

Even the thought of Pierce's mum setting him up with someone caused a bone deep ache to settle inside me. I know it can't be easy sneaking around, but I still want to be with him. The thought of him with another woman causes a fury to ignite inside me that I can't contain.

"Sorry for all the questions. The children have been cooped up inside because of all the rain," the director tells me.

"No worries. I'm sure they're all ready to get home."

We finish the tour, and the director curtsies to me as we leave. The press is stationed outside, as usual.

"Was today a good visit, Princess Charlotte?"

"Any update on your love life?"

I give a polite wave, before heading into the safety of the awaiting car. I wish I could snap my fingers and just do away with everyone asking me about my love life. I should be used to it by now, but it's hitting harder than usual.

All I want is to find Pierce and curl up next to him. Bounce ideas off of him for my charity. Hold his hand in public and tell everyone that we're dating. Take him to events where I can show off what an incredible man he is.

But no. We're subject to late night dates at his place, where I can sneak in and out without the press finding out. All because the Queen needs to keep a firm grasp on the royal family.

Needing his calming voice, I pick up the phone and dial him immediately.

"Hey, love." He picks up on the first ring.

"Hi." I let out a deep breath I didn't realize I was holding. His voice is instantly calming.

"Everything okay?" The sound of the tattoo guns fades away, as a door clicks shut through the phone.

"Just needed to hear your voice."

He chuckles to himself. "Anything I can do to help. How was your morning?"

"Any chance you can get away this weekend?" I blurt out, ignoring his question.

"What, like a holiday?"

"Yes. Just a short weekend away from the city. You. Me. No press. Just be together without any interference from anyone else."

"What happened this morning?" His voice is concerned.

I can't blame him. "Just your average morning. Kids asking if I'll meet my prince. The press asking about my love life. I'm sick of it. I just want to be with you."

"How does Bibury sound? We can sneak away to my family's cottage we have there. No one is there this time of year. Just you and me." Pierce doesn't hesitate.

"Sounds like heaven." I settle farther back into the seat as we race through London.

"Perfect. A weekend away, just the two of us."

I could cry at how beautiful those words sound. Just Pierce and me together. It's music to my ears.

Shoreditch
INK

Chapter Seventeen

PIERCE

"So this is your family house?" Charlotte's eyes are wide as I pull up to the cottage in Bibury. Her smile is bright.

I nod my head. "We came here during summer holidays if we weren't visiting Mum's family. And celebrated every Christmas here."

"It's beautiful." Leaves are falling off the trees that line the front of the stone house.

"Wait until you see inside." I grab her hand, kissing her knuckles. "Let's go."

Charlotte's security officers came up earlier to ensure everything was safe. Not something I've ever experienced, but if it means we get to spend the weekend together, I'll suck it up.

"Can we move here?" Charlotte's voice is a whisper as we walk into the house. Wood beams cover the low ceiling. A small sofa sits in front of the fireplace. The kitchen takes up the back of the first floor before stairs lead up to the bedrooms. "This is perfect."

Charlotte walks up to me, grabbing my cheeks and

pulling me down for a kiss. It's soft. The barest hint of a tease. When she pulls back, her eyes are glassy.

"You alright, love?" I wrap my arm around her waist, tugging her into me.

She sighs, relaxing into my touch. "It's just been a hard few weeks. I hate having to hide what we have."

I drop a kiss on her head, breathing in the scent of her shampoo. God, this woman consumes me. Every thought, every feeling, every touch. "It's worth it. I know it sucks, but if it means I get to be with you, I'd hide out in every closet just to see you or touch you."

She turns, resting her chin on my chest and gazing up at me. "Aren't you just a charmer today?"

I smirk down at her, tucking a loose strand of hair behind her ear. "C'mon. I want to show you all the favourite parts of the village."

"Does one of them happen to be your room?" Charlotte waggles her eyebrows at me. Fucking hell, my dick is twitching in my pants.

"No. As much as I'd love to show you the bedroom,"—I drop a kiss on her lips—"there's a lot of fun things about this place that I love."

Charlotte straightens before me, grabbing her wide-brimmed hat and dropping it on her head. "I'm at your every whim today. Show me the Bibury you love."

God, I love this woman. I don't know how she feels, but I've gone and fallen in love with the woman that I'm not supposed to be seeing. Everything about her has pulled me in. Her laugh. Her smile. The way she lights up when she talks about the work she does. My heart beats for her. I want to do everything I can to make her life easier.

Because maybe we might get to be together someday. For real. Maybe. Hopefully?

Charlotte's tugging me out of the house, but I lead her to the side shed. "We're not walking?"

I laugh as I throw the doors open. "We're biking. Best way to see the entire village."

"I don't think I've ridden a bike in years."

"Good thing it's like riding a bike then."

She smacks my chest. "Aren't you the funny one."

I capture her lips with mine before hopping onto my bike. "I try. Now, let's go."

It's cold, but not as cold as it could be, as we start off towards town. Charlotte's security officers are following behind us in my car. Not the most obvious, but she still has to have them. I peek back at Charlotte, and the brightest smile paints her face. I feel it in my chest. Happiness is radiating off of her as she pedals behind me.

"This is fantastic!" she shouts at me. The old houses of Arlington Row pass by in a blur as we head farther into the small town. The river winds by on the other side, acting as our guide. I turn, finding one of the small footbridges to stop next to.

"Enjoying yourself?" I'm straddling the bike as Charlotte stops beside me.

"I get to stare at your cute arse. Of course I'm enjoying myself."

I shake my head at her. "And here I thought you were enjoying the town."

Charlotte grabs the lapels of my coat, bringing my face down to hers. "I'm enjoying myself because I'm with you. We could be in a shack on the sea, and it'd be fab. Your cute bum is just a plus."

I slant my lips over hers, licking into her mouth—needing to feel close to her. Her lips are cold from the wind. "Want to head into the coffee shop and warm up?"

Her eyes are hazy as she pulls back. "Mm, a tea sounds perfect right now."

We steer our bikes away from the footbridge and towards the small village. The main part of town has only a few shops, and even fewer people, so it's perfect for us. Charlotte tucks into a back booth as I grab us each a cuppa.

"Cheers." I clink my glass against hers.

Charlotte sips on hers, keeping her eyes on me. "Thank you for bringing me here. I didn't realize how much I needed to get away." Her hand lands on top of mine.

"It sucks not being able to tell people we're together, but I'm glad we're here. Even if only for a few days."

Charlotte's face is pensive as she looks at me. "The only weekend getaways we had when we were younger were to Sandringham. There's a small town there, but everyone knew us, so it's not like we could escape like here. I don't think one person has noticed me."

There's an older couple sitting at a table by the window, but no one else. "That's one of the perks. It's a small village. There were a few other kids here growing up, but it was mainly always Sean and me playing by ourselves."

"I can only imagine what it would've been like coming here as a kid."

"Yeah, but think of the places you got to see growing up. Not a lot of people could have travelled like that."

"I have a good life." Charlotte rests her chin in her hand, staring back at me. "But you still see a very polished version of wherever you go. They don't want you to see the bad bits."

I link my hand with her free one. "I guess I never thought of it like that."

"People only see what they want to see. It's a very

glamorised life, and it's mostly good. But people don't understand the hard parts."

"Like?"

"Like wanting to be with someone so badly, but you can't and have to hide it."

My heart aches for her. I want to shout it from the rooftops that we're together. That we love each other. But the idea that it could be a scandal is hard. We've been careful together. So careful. Even now, my eyes keep drifting to see if anyone has a camera.

"I want nothing more than to kiss you and hug you in public. But until then, I'm happy to be with you anyway I can."

Charlotte leans in for a kiss, tasting like the tea she's been sipping on. "You make me happy. So, so happy." Her breath is a whisper against my lips.

"And I'd do anything to keep you happy. Like bringing you to our family home in the tiniest village in England."

Charlotte lets out a quiet laugh. "Fordwich is actually the smallest town in England."

I roll my eyes at her, finishing my tea. "Of course you would know that."

"What can I say?" She shrugs her shoulders. "I know a lot of obscure facts about this country."

"Maybe we could find a way to go to a quiz night at the pub. You'd clean up there."

Charlotte laces her warm fingers through mine. "Consider it a date then."

WE TAKE the long way back to the cottage, stopping at the river for no other reason than to watch it float by. Kissing. Touching. I love seeing Bibury through Charlotte's eyes. I've only ever come up here with family. No one has ever been special enough to bring here.

But Charlotte? I'd buy the entire town if it meant we could be together for real.

We drop our bikes off in the shed and head into the warmth of the house. "Want to get started on dinner?" My hands drift around Charlotte's back, warming up under her jumper. She squirms under my touch.

"You're mean!" She shimmies away from me, heading towards the kitchen. "Why don't you start the fire and I'll start dinner. I had the guys get everything I need to make you my special dinner."

"Special dinner? That sounds promising."

She strips off her hat and jumper, standing in a tight tank top. "Yes. So get comfortable, get us some drinks, and I'll make you a meal you'll never forget."

I don't think it's the meal that will be unforgettable, but the woman making it. Her eyes are sparkling with happiness as she leaves me to it.

I stoke the fire as the clattering of pans drifts out of the kitchen. Charlotte's soft voice is singing. It brings a smile to my face, one I rarely feel. That anxiousness at never being good enough falls away when I'm with her. I don't have to live up to any crazy expectations when I'm with Charlotte. We can just be.

With the fire started, I head into the kitchen to find the woman who is bringing me to life. Her dark brown locks are swept into a knot on the top of her head, and her cheeks are pink from the heat of the stove.

"How's it going?"

She turns her dark brown eyes on me, apron now tied around her waist. "It's going. Pour us some wine."

I brush by her as I grab the wine glasses. "Smells good," I whisper into her ear.

"Stop distracting me." She elbows me out of the way.

"Sorry. Anything I can do to help?" I pour us each a glass of red.

"Grab the veggies from the refrigerator so I can start on the sauce."

Getting what she needs, I hand everything over. Meat is simmering in a pot as spaghetti boils in another. "Spaghetti?"

"Hey." Her eyes swing to me, poking towards me with the knife in her hand. "It's the best damn spaghetti you'll ever have. A chef in Italy taught me how to make this sauce."

I wrap my arms around her shoulders. "I can't wait to have the Charlotte special." I drop a kiss on her nose before pulling back, not wanting to distract her. Charlotte's smile is happy as she goes back to cooking. I settle on a barstool, watching as she works. Her hips shake as she cuts and stirs, her hands moving quickly to slice the veggies as she makes the sauce. I move to set the small table, not wanting to be a useless wanker.

It's intoxicating, being swept up in this woman's world. We might not have a lot of moments together, but I cherish the ones we do get. And I'll love getting to wake up beside her tomorrow, holding her in my arms. It's the thing I hate most about this arrangement.

"We just need to let the sauce sit for a bit and then dinner will be ready." Hair is plastered to Charlotte's fore-head, face red from cooking.

"Cooking looks good on you."

"Wait until you try it." Charlotte takes off the apron,

setting it on the counter. "I promise, best meal you'll ever have."

"It'll be the best meal I'll ever have because you made it for me, love."

Charlotte's hand captures my chin, locking eyes with me. "You are such a charmer, you know that?" She brushes her lips against mine. "I don't know what I'm going to do with you, Pierce."

My eyebrows waggle at her. "Feed me and then I'll show you a thing or two."

Chapter Eighteen

CHARLOTTE

"I have a surprise for you today." Pierce's lips dance up my spine as he wakes me up. His voice is heavy with sleep. I never realised how good it feels to wake up next to someone. Going to bed with Pierce felt pretty good too.

"What kind of surprise?" I sit up, pulling the sheet with me. Pierce's hair is standing on end. Pillow lines decorate his face. We gave each other several orgasms last night and then passed out in spectacular fashion.

"If I told you, it wouldn't be a surprise. Now, get dressed and meet me downstairs." He pops out of bed, his fine arse on full display for me.

I drop the sheet, crawling on my knees over to Pierce. "I'm going to shower. Care to join me?" I drag my fingers across his chest as I saunter into the bathroom. His hurried footsteps are quick to join me.

"ROLLER SKATING?" My eyes are lit up with excitement at the bright pink roller skates in his hand. After a not so short shower together, Pierce dragged me downstairs for my surprise. He was like a kid at Christmas. He couldn't contain his excitement.

"I figure we can unleash that inner derby girl."

I can't help it; I jump into his arms and lay kisses all over his face. "This might be one of the most fun things anyone has ever done for me."

I've never told anyone about my desire to be a roller girl. When you grow up as a princess, you're not allowed to have dreams like regular people. We were raised in the royal ways and how to put our best foot forward. Always.

Wanting to roller skate? I would've been laughed at if I told people this was something I always wanted to do. But not Pierce. He went out and bought me a pair of skates and is going to spend the morning with me while I roller skate. What did I do to deserve someone as good as him?

Pierce squeezes my hip before setting me down. "I aim to please. Now, let's get going because I can't wait to see you in skates."

Walking outside to the small driveway, I find a typical cold and grey day. There's not much room to skate, but seeing as how I've only done this a handful of times, I won't need much space.

"Are you going to catch me if I fall?"

Pierce quirks a brow at me. "Have you ever done this before?"

I shove my socked feet into the skates. A perfect fit. "Only a few times as a kid. I wasn't the most coordinated of kids, so I think they didn't want me breaking any bones."

"Are you going to be breaking any bones today?"

I tie the bright green laces and reach out to Pierce to stand. "That's not the plan."

Steady hands lead me away from the bench as we start to move over the uneven surface.

"You know you actually have to use your feet to skate, right?"

"Feck off, you. It's not like riding a bike."

"Sorry. You're doing wonderful, and you'd win the Olympic medal of skating."

I tighten my grip on his hands, keeping my eyes on his feet. "No need to flatter me. I know I'm not going to be good at this."

"How about this." Pierce rolls me into his arms, wrapping me in his warmth. "For each lap you take around the driveway, I'll give you a kiss?" He drops a soft kiss on the corner of my mouth.

I eye him warily. "And what was that one for? Good luck?"

"You don't want my incentive?" He mocks being annoyed. "I'll have you know that's the best possible motivation to learn to skate."

I'm closer to eye level with Pierce in my skates. "I can think of a much better motivation than a kiss." I dip my hands under his jumper, warming my cold hands on his hot skin.

"Orgasms for laps? I guess I could get on board with that." An innocent smile stretches across Pierce's lips.

"Good." I shove Pierce out of my arms before he can give me another brain-swirling kiss. "Now, out of my way while I become the world's best skater."

It would've been a much more convincing statement had I not pushed off and immediately fallen on my arse. Pierce is doubled over in laughter. He goes to help me up, but I wave him off.

"No help! I want to earn my orgasms on my own."

"Alright, love. I'll just be sitting here watching you go."

I flip him the bird as I stand like a baby giraffe for the first time. This was much easier when I was trying to do it as a child.

Pushing off on each foot, I get a little momentum, circling part of the drive. Pierce's face is twisted in laughter. His laughter only makes me more determined.

Getting the hang of it, I take a turn and move slower than a turtle back to him. "Look at me go!" I throw my arms up in victory as I pass him.

"You'll be trying out for the Olympics in no time," he says dryly, his arms crossed over his chest as he watches me take another lap.

Turning on my next lap, I get cocky, and my foot catches on a rock. Thrashing my arms, I try to balance myself, but end up falling face first in the grass. "Shite!"

"Are you alright?" Pierce is on top of me as I flip over, laughter bubbling out of me.

"Why did I ever think I could be a roller girl? I'm bloody awful at this!" Deep, belly laughs take over. Pierce's face goes from one of concern to echoing my laugh.

"I'm glad you said it and not me." Pierce's voice is breathy with laughter. "And here I thought you'd be skating laps around me."

"Hey! I got in one lap. Even that incentive didn't do much, did it?" I pop a brow at him.

"Oh I don't know." He pulls my feet into his lap, untying the laces. "I could be convinced that you're sad your dream died today and make it up to you."

"Pierce. I'm so sad. I'll never be a roller girl, and I don't know what to do with my life," I say, dramatics lacing my tone.

"Poor Charlotte. However will I make it up to you?"

His eyes darken with need. He yanks the skates off my feet. As I wiggle my toes, he digs his knuckles into the arches of my feet.

"Mm. That feels amazing." I lie back on the cold grass, the morning sky still foggy around us. "I feel that we should go try to surf now."

"Charlotte, I say this with all the kindness I possess, but what makes you think you'll be able to surf?"

I poke his hard chest with my toe. "I meant for you. There's no way I'm ever getting on a surfboard."

"Alright then." Pierce lies down beside me, pulling me closer to him. "Where do you suggest we run off to and try to surf?"

"The river looked nice." I smirk at him.

"My balls would shrivel up and fall off if we even set a toe in that river. You're crazy, love!" A full body shiver wracks over him.

"Fine." I fist my hands in his jumper, pulling him closer. "But how about the next time we escape the city, we go somewhere warm, and you can try your hand at surfing?"

Pierce pulls me closer to him as he rolls onto his back. I throw a leg over his, cuddling into his side. The cold of the grass fades away as I'm wrapped up in his warmth.

"I like that idea. Learning how to surf. Lazing about on the beach. I can't remember the last time I've been on a true holiday."

"This is shaping up to be a pretty good one." I tilt my chin, gazing up at his handsome face. He's staring at me like he doesn't have a care in the world. That there is no other place he'd rather be. That watching me face plant in epic fashion on a pair of skates is how he wants to spend every morning.

"I'm glad you brought me here. This is just what I needed."

"I'll bring you here every weekend if it means we get to be together without the prying eyes of the world wanting to tear us apart."

"I hate that it has to be this way."

"I know, love, I know. But I'd do it a hundred times over if it means I get to be with you."

I don't know why Pierce thinks I'm worth it. Why putting up with my royal life is worth it. My last ex couldn't handle it. And he was someone the Queen approved of.

Now, here's a man who is putting up with sneaking around and we can't be together in a way I truly want. I want to shout our relationship from the rooftops and tell everyone how wonderful a partner he could be for me. I know he struggles with playing second fiddle to his brother and would hate for him to feel that way with me. But his words and actions do nothing but support me. He is the kindest, most caring man I've ever met.

Falling in love with someone you're hiding away isn't easy. It's getting harder and harder to keep our relationship a secret. I don't know how we'll get to stay together, but I'm going to do everything in my power to keep Pierce. Because he's the one.

I only hope he feels the same way about me.

Chapter Nineteen

CHARLOTTE

"Okay, next question," Pierce says, as he settles above me, leaning on his elbow. After another fantastic supper, we made a fort of blankets in front of the fire. I'm in nothing but his shirt, Pierce only in joggers. It feels like we're kids again, hiding from the world. Not a worry in sight of who is trying to keep us apart.

"You really like these questions, don't you?" I ask, tracing my fingers over his chest. The strong muscles ripple under my touch. I love seeing the reaction I cause in him. It stirs something deep inside me, knowing that this man craves my touch in a way no man ever has before.

"Yes. I don't think we've come even close to twenty." Pierce drops a chaste kiss on my lips, making no move to deepen it. "I'll never tire of your questions. Hit me."

"Where do you see yourself in five years?"

Pierce scrubs a hand over his stubbly jaw. "Are you my secondary counsellor? Asking what I see in my future?"

"It's a valid question." My fingers move lower, tracing the intricate ink that runs down his side. "My future has been planned out for me since before I was born."

"Does it ever bother you that you never had a choice?" Pierce's words are soft, the rippling fire the only other sound in the small cottage.

"When I was a moody teenager, yes. I thought the world would end if I had to be told what to do and where to be my entire life. That's when I went through my stage of wearing all black."

Pierce laughs, his fingers drifting down my stomach. "I can't imagine you being a sullen teenager. You're the happiest person I've ever met."

"It's not like I was likely going to ever become Queen, but I thought my life was over. It wasn't until I went to uni that I realized what a privileged position I'm in. How I want to make a mark in this world by creating my own charity."

"You will, Charlotte." Pierce's fingers drift over my cheek. "You've done incredible work on planning the women's charity, and I know it'll do great things for so many people."

Something settles in my chest. People always tell me how much my work means to them. That I make a difference in their lives. I hear it so often, that sometimes it's hard to believe. But when Pierce says it, it's as if everything settles into place. It's not a given yet, but it's affirming to hear Pierce say these words to me. Almost like the Queen can't say no. Won't say no.

"What are you thinking about, love?"

My fingers wind into the hair at the nape of his neck. His eyes are bright, the fire sparkling in them, his square jaw firm as he takes me in. "Just how happy I am to be here with you. You have no idea how much I needed this weekend."

Pierce lies on his side, shifting me so I'm looking directly into his eyes. "I hate how this is the only time I can wake up with you in my arms. All I want is to hold you every morning. Wake up beside you."

I trace my fingers over his plump lips. Lips that have brought me so much happiness. "Is that where you see yourself in five years? Waking up with me?"

His hand is firm on my hip, his eyes serious. "What would a future for the two of us look like? Would I be called Prince Pierce?" There's a lightness to his tone that belies the serious look on his face.

That piece that settled inside me feels like it's moving around in my chest. A living, breathing thing that threatens to ruin this happy bubble we're in.

"Yes. You'd be in the spotlight. Cameras thrust in your face every day. Your face plastered all across magazines across the world. Every move you make documented. People wanting to get tattoos from the famous Pierce."

"Is that all?" He chuckles. "Piece of cake."

"I'm serious. My last serious relationship ended because he couldn't handle the spotlight. Couldn't handle being a step behind me for the rest of our lives. The first time his photo was in a newspaper, I could see the struggle. He hated it, but it was as if he didn't know what to do. We were together a long time after that, but every day was hard. I was selfish and didn't want to end it. I thought I had finally found my person. But he left me high and dry."

"A lesser man then. I could never leave you like that. Would never leave you like that." He moves his hand off my hip and cups my face. His thumb gently strokes the apple of my cheek. "He didn't see how incredible you really are, Charlotte. The way you light up when you talk about your work. It brings out something incredible in you. That you want to serve your people like you do."

A few weeks with Pierce, and it's like he knows exactly what to say to me. Anytime I met someone, I compared them to Michael. Would they be as strong as him? Would they run scared before we even made it past a second date? One date with Pierce, and we were front page news. He's taken it all in stride, but for how much longer?

"I know it'll be hard, but we can make it work, can't we?" His words break me out of my thoughts.

I sigh, my breath ghosting his cheeks. He's moved closer to me, his skin hot on mine. "You know what it was like for Ellie. She gave up the throne to have what she really wanted in life. It's a sacrifice so few people would be willing to make. And Zara had a hard go of it, and she's the daughter of a duke."

"If it means I would get to have you by my side, it's a sacrifice I'd be willing to make."

I shove off of him, trying to lighten the mood. "You say that now. It's very different when the entire kingdom is bearing down on you."

"I've never had an entire kingdom's future on my shoulders. Could be fun to try."

This man. If he doesn't make my heart beat for him. "We'd just have to get your official seal of approval from the Queen."

"Are there prince lessons I could take? If so, sign me up." Pierce wraps me in his arms.

"Here's your first lesson." I push him back on the pile of blankets underneath our fort, straddling his hips. "What the princess wants, the princess gets."

A heated gaze sends shivers down my body. "That one is easy. What do I get for passing your lesson?"

I quirk my lips at him, his arms now propped behind his head. "I can think of an incentive." I drop hot, open-mouthed kisses down his chest, licking the swirl of colours on his pecs. When I draw the tight bud of his nipple into my mouth, he hisses.

"Damn, Charlotte. You know just how to make a man feel good."

"You'll be feeling really good." I move down his body, drawing his joggers down his thighs. His thick cock springs free, a bead of precum on the crown. I wrap my hand around the base, licking the white bead.

"Fuck, Charlotte." Pierce fists my hair in one hand, gently holding my head as I take him as far as I can. His hips jerk off the floor as I work his cock in tandem with my hand. I love taking Pierce like this. Feeling his need for me. Feeling him come apart under my touch is a powerful feeling and turns me on even more.

Pierce's hips move faster as he starts to fuck my mouth. My eyes well with tears, but I make no move to leave. I let him use my mouth. It's a heady sensation. The raw passion swirling around us pushes me closer to my own orgasm.

"Shit. I'm going to come." Pierce moves to pull me off of him, but I suck him down farther as the first spurts of his cum land on my tongue. I drink him up, loving the taste of his salty release. I take every last drop before pulling off of him.

"Is this what prince lessons are like?" His voice comes out on a huff, his chest rising and falling as he comes down from his high. I wipe the corners of my lips on the back of my hand. I pull his pants back up, as I settle my weight over his chest.

"With this princess, yes."

"Can I sign up for daily lessons?"

"I do lessons by the hour if that pleases you." I walk my fingers up his chest, then trace the features of his sexy face. I can't get enough of this man.

"Shit. Is death by sex a thing? Because I reckon you'll kill me if we do that."

The tight need in my core is bordering on painful. Bringing Pierce pleasure like that has me on the edge.

"If I don't get your mouth on me, I might die right now." Overdramatic, yes. But his lips landing on mine as he flips me over has me climbing closer and closer towards the edge of the cliff.

"You know, these prince lessons are easy. If you're going to quiz me, you should at least make it harder." Pierce draws his shirt up my body, exposing my bare pussy to him. The soft brush of his hands over my stomach has me arching into his touch.

"You seem to be catching on very quickly."

Pierce flattens his tongue against my slit, dragging through the wetness building there. "What can I say? I'm a quick study." The pressure of his tongue has me bucking my hips, riding his face. His strong hands hold my legs apart.

"Mm, Pierce. Just like that." My voice is rough, laced with need. Need for this man. His tongue is working my clit. Soft strokes. Hard strokes. Fast then slow. Heat is racing down my spine, an inferno ready to explode.

"You like my tongue? Or do you want my fingers too?" Pierce slowly, oh so slowly, sinks a thick finger inside my pussy. He crooks it, hitting that delicious spot deep inside me.

"I'm so close, Pierce. So close."

Pierce thrusts two fingers inside me, swiping his tongue over my clit. "I need you to come. I want to taste you on my tongue. Feel the way you use my mouth as you climax. Over and over again."

His words.

His fingers.

His tongue.

They drive a soul-shattering orgasm out of me. Stars

burst behind my eyes as I ride his face. The world could be ending, and I wouldn't know. Because right now, it's only Pierce and me, in this tiny cottage in Bibury.

My muscles shake as I come down from my high. My body is boneless. Pierce settles over me, a hand on each side of my head. My release glistens on his lips. He drops a kiss on my lips, but when he goes to pull away, I pull him back. The taste of me on his tongue is hot. Mix it with his release on mine, and it's downright sinful. Our tongues fight for control, but our bodies are languid. Sated after each of our releases. My legs wrap around his, keeping him close.

"Damn, Charlotte." Pierce shifts back from me, breaking the kiss. "That was the hottest fucking thing I've ever seen."

A satisfied grin plays on my lips. "It's only because of you."

Pierce growls. "Fuck. You know just what to say to turn me on." He rolls his hips into my core, his cock already hardening.

"Consider me the Pierce whisperer then."

"I love that you know exactly what I like. Fuck, it's so damn sexy having a woman who knows exactly what she wants and takes it. And gives it too."

"I should say the same about you. You know just what to say and do to make me feel so lo…treasured."

I know I love this man, but it's hard to get the words to come out. The words came easily with Michael. He was supposed to be my forever, but he cut and ran. I want Pierce. I want him with an ache that I've never felt before.

So why is it so damn hard to say those three little words to him?

Chapter Twenty

CHARLOTTE

"Why do I have to keep my eyes closed?" My hands are covering my eyes as Pierce moves around in front of me.

"Because it's a surprise. I promise, you'll love it."

"It smells like hot cocoa." The air smells sweet.

"Stop trying to guess."

We haven't left our blanket fort all night. We've spent our time here talking. About everything and anything. About my charity. About his work. I want to soak up every second with Pierce before going back to real life.

"Okay, open your eyes."

Pierce is sitting next to me with…something in his hands? "What is this?" I take it from Pierce's hand.

"Try it. I promise, you'll love it."

I take a big bite of whatever this is that is melting.

"This might be the best thing I've ever put in my mouth."

"That's what she said," Pierce says, a smirk covering his face.

"I don't even care. Why have I never had this before?" Gooey marshmallow drips from my fingers as I take another bite.

"S'mores. They aren't a thing here. We used to have them when we visited my grandparents over summer holiday. They are my favourite."

Pierce takes another large bite, his eyes glittering with happiness. The joy shining out from him is like a light in my chest. I've never been this content before.

"I command you make these for me all the time."

He pulls me onto his lap. "You command me to?"

I rest an elbow on his shoulder, taking the last bite of this delicious treat. "I'm a princess. I can command you to do my bidding."

Heat flares in his eyes. "Is that right?"

I nod, licking my lips. "Yes. I command you make me s'mores every night from here on out."

Pierce grabs my hand before I can lick the sticky goo off my fingers, sucking them into his mouth, his eyes now dark with need. Heat floods my core as his tongue circles the pads of my fingers.

"Can you also command me to do other things?" He pulls my fingers out of his mouth, kissing down my arm. My pulse is racing beneath his lips.

"Like to fuck me right here on the floor?"

A growl escapes his lips before they crash into mine. He tastes like marshmallows and chocolate and Pierce. I rise on my knees, deepening the angle of the kiss. I want this man with a fire I've never known.

Pierce's hands drift up my stomach, his fingers ghosting my breasts. A low moan escapes as he tweaks a nipple between his fingers. His lips move down my jaw, my neck, before he rips the shirt off of me, leaving me completely exposed to him.

"Fecking hell, you're the most gorgeous woman I've ever laid eyes on." Pierce's words cause my heart to stutter in my chest. This man. I don't know what I did to deserve him.

His hands roam over my body, fire left in their wake. "God, I need you." Desire drips from my voice as his lips take my nipple into his mouth. I rock over his erection, throbbing beneath me. I'm shameless as I grind over him. Pierce moves to my other breast, lavishing it with the same attention.

My hands drift lower, his chest flexing beneath them as my fingers skirt the waist band of his joggers. Pierce pulls the taut bud of my nipple into his mouth as I dive my hands into his joggers, meeting the hard flesh of his cock.

"Fuck," he moans on a long breath. He throws his head back in pleasure as I brush my fingers over him.

His hands drift up my thighs, his thumbs grazing my clit. It lights an inferno in me. "I need you inside me, Pierce."

Pierce flips us around, laying me out on the soft blankets. The orange light from the fire casts him in a gentle glow. He's studying my face like I'm studying his. Memorising it. Taking in every feature lest we forget one another.

His lips meet mine in a sensual kiss. Pierce's tongue demands control, and I willingly give it. The powerful, yet languid, strokes cause a fire to burn low in my belly. Heat floods my core as he deepens the kiss.

I've never been kissed like this before. Like a merging of two souls. I lean into Pierce's touch, craving more of his lips on mine and needing his hands on me. Using my feet, I shove his joggers down his legs. I want to feel every bare inch of his body on mine.

Pierce's lips move down my neck. Hot, open-mouthed kisses nibble at my skin and at the swell of my breasts before he pulls a diamond hard nipple into his mouth. My hands fist in his hair, keeping him there. His teeth and tongue are working me into a frenzy.

"Pierce. Please." My voice is breathy, coming out on a long moan as Pierce shifts to my other nipple.

"Not yet, love." His eyes drift up to mine as he toys with the tight bud, swirling his tongue before taking it in his mouth. I can't keep my eyes off him. He knows how to bring me pleasure as if he were a professor studying my body.

His hands drift lower, swiping through my slick folds. I arch into his touch. I want his cock, but his fingers on my clit ratchet my pleasure up. The mix of pressure is dizzying. My orgasm is racing down my spine, just out of reach.

I'm writhing with need as Pierce slips a finger inside me. His lips smile against my hot skin as he works his way down my stomach. "God, I can't wait to feel you come on my tongue." Pierce's voice is gravelly with need as he tongues my clit.

"Please. I'm so close," I beg. I'm needy and wanting and don't care how desperate I sound. "I need to come."

"What are you waiting for?" Pierce sucks down on my clit as he starts thrusting his fingers in faster, pulling me over the edge.

It's an orgasm like I've never felt before. The intensity racks my body. It's powerful in the way it colours my vision and slows time. Like Pierce and I are the only two people on earth.

Pierce's lips on mine bring me back to reality. My body is still high on his as I taste my release on his lips. "I've never seen anything so beautiful as when you come." His voice is heavy with reverence. His hands worship my body as he shifts us to our sides. Pierce grabs the condom from his sweats, but I still him.

"No. I'm clean, and I want to feel you, all of you, inside of me."

"Christ, Charlotte. I'm clean too." Pierce takes my mouth in a hot kiss, his tongue stroking over mine.

Pulling my leg over his hip, Pierce notches his cock at my entrance. Wrapping my arms around him, I bring him closer, feeling him slip inside. His eyes don't leave mine as he sinks all the way.

I bite down on my lip. The pleasure is already so intense from my earlier orgasm. Pierce's eyes are hooded with a desire that matches my own.

"You feel incredible. Fuck, I don't think anything will compare to this." He sets a slow pace, his thrusts steady and measured. An ache to be closer to him washes over me as I bring him nearer to me. His forehead drops to mine as he squeezes me to him.

This isn't sex. This is making love. This is slow and passionate and everything I've always dreamed of. This connection, this unspoken connection, with another person that binds you to them.

I feel it with Pierce. Every touch, every word, every kiss.

"Charlotte." His voice is needy as I start to feel the pulses of his release. It takes me over the edge with him. He buries his face in my neck as we ride out our orgasms together.

The stillness in the air surrounds us, lying wrapped up in one another. Pierce pulls out and takes me in his arms. The only sound is the fire crackling. His fingers drift down my spine. I've never felt more at peace. A blissed-out smile spreads on my face as the slow steady rhythm of Pierce's heart pulls me under.

IT'S EARLY. Or late. I'm not sure what time it is when I wake up. The fire is out, and I'm wrapped around Pierce like a koala. His breathing is easy, his hand clutching mine to his chest. We're lying mixed up on the blankets and pillows. It's dark out, and a howling wind cuts through the quiet of the small cottage.

Things are perfect right now with Pierce. This weekend away was exactly what we needed. It's been a hard few weeks with the pressure of hiding our relationship from those closest to us. And it'll get even harder these next few weeks with the holidays coming up.

I try not to think about the future of our relationship. This sweet, thoughtful, tattooed man is everything I've ever wanted. He didn't think twice when I asked him to keep our relationship a secret. All I want, all I crave, is to be able to share our love with the world.

But tomorrow we go back to the real world. The real world won't care that we want to be together. Pierce stirs next to me, his heavy breaths ghosting my face.

He's the most beautiful man I've ever seen. Long eyelashes. Defined jaw. Plump lips. I never want to be without this man, but the longer we're in hiding, the stronger I sense that we're somehow moving closer to imploding.

The thought is so terrible, it steels something inside of me. I can't let Pierce go. There has to be a middle ground we can find. To be together and still support the Queen's work. Nothing will be figured out tonight. All I can do is enjoy these last few hours away with Pierce and hope that whatever plan I come up with allows us to be together.

Because I can't lose him.
It has to work.
It just has to.

Shoreditch
INK

Chapter Twenty-One

PIERCE

"**W**hat the actual fuck, Pierce?"

Ellie comes waddling into the shop, her belly making an appearance before her.

"What are you talking about, Pink?" I'm cleaning my station after my last appointment of the day.

"This." She thrusts a paper in my arms, her pink hair a wild halo around her head. On the front cover is a picture of Charlotte and me leaving the cafe in Bibury.

Princess Charlotte has a new love interest. See page 5 for all the details.

FUCK. Fuck, fuck, fuck! We were careful. No one in Bibury cares about status, so I thought we were safe. We couldn't be seen together, or the Queen would be furious. Shit.

"Care to explain any of this?" Ellie's words break through the chaos swirling in my head. I can only stare at her. I flip to the designated page, and across the entire magazine is pictures from our weekend away. Pictures from biking. Sitting along the river. Kisses in front of the cafe. What I thought was a safe trip could end up destroying Charlotte. Destroying what we have.

"I need to talk to Charlotte." I push past Ellie, heading to the back offices. Sean is restocking supplies when I brush by him.

"How did I not know you two were seeing each other?" Ellie calls after me.

"Who's seeing each other?" Sean asks, his gaze moving between Ellie and me.

"Charlotte and Pierce."

"I thought you were setting Charlotte up with someone?" Sean's eyebrows furrow in confusion. I love my brother, but sometimes he can be a real wanker.

"For fuck's sake, Sean. We were seeing each other," I belt out.

He turns to Ellie. "Did you know?"

She shakes her head. "No, but now the entire world does." She hands Sean the magazine, and he looks at it before turning back to me.

"What in the world have you done?"

Anger boils out of me. "Oh, so I'm the only one who can't date who he wants to? Only you two are allowed to do that?" I wave my finger between the two of them.

"That's not fair, Pierce." Ellie's voice is quiet when she looks at me, a blush spreading across her face.

"Yeah, well, it's pretty unfucking fair from where I'm standing. You two can be together, but Charlotte and I can't?" I'm pacing the tiny space. All I want to do is talk to Charlotte, but who knows if that's even possible now.

Ellie grabs my arm, halting my movements. "It's different. I'm no longer a princess. She is. There's a different standard."

Ellie's words cut deep. "Wow. Thanks for thinking I'm not good enough for Charlotte."

Her face turns soft, and Sean comes to stand behind her. "It's not that at all. When you're a royal, you don't always get a say in the matter."

"How did we not know about this?" Sean asks.

I scrub my hands over my jaw. "We were being careful." Sean snorts.

"Seriously?" I'm ready to punch my brother in the face.

Ellie turns to Sean, giving him a similar look to mine. "Can you give us a minute?"

He drops a kiss on her forehead and heads out front. "What's your goal here, Pierce? Is this some fling? Are you in love? What?"

Ellie crosses her arms, piercing me with a punishing stare. It's the face that says *I may not be a princess anymore, but I can still get what I want out of you.*

"Of course she's more than a fling." I'm fucking in love with the woman, but I don't want to tell her cousin that before I tell her. "We wouldn't be sneaking around if it were a fling."

"So then what do you plan on doing?"

"Can I not just fucking talk to Charlotte first?" I boom. I can't control the anger bubbling up inside me. "Look, I'm sorry, Ellie. But I just can't be here right now. Tell Sean I'll see him tomorrow."

"Wait, Pierce!" I don't give Ellie another glance as I leave the shop. Pulling out my phone, I dial Charlotte's number immediately. It goes straight to voicemail. Fuck. This can't be good.

Charlotte

NOTHING LIKE GETTING a summons from the Queen first thing in the morning. A lead weight settled in my stomach from the time I left my apartment to getting here at the palace. The knowing faces of the staff tell me whatever I was called here for can't be good. And she's making me wait.

"Your Highness. Her Majesty will see you now." The Queen's advisor opens the door to her office, allowing me to enter.

"Thank you." Nervous energy is crackling through the air. Or maybe it's just my nerves.

"Charlotte. Thank you for coming on such short notice." Aunt Katherine is sitting behind her desk, looking every bit the regal Queen she is this morning.

"What was so urgent that it couldn't wait?" I take a seat in front of her, my hands twisting in my lap.

"I wanted to talk to you about this." She throws down several magazines and newspapers on the desk in front of me. All of them have Pierce and me on the front page of the paper. Forget nerves. Every terrible feeling I had of being found out is crashing into me. I can't hear anything around me. I can only focus on the images in front of me. Of Pierce and me in Bibury. Of us sneaking off to the cafe. Stolen kisses.

"Do you have anything to say for yourself?" The tight draw of her face sticks me harder than I thought. No words come out.

"Did you honestly think you could get away with this? The press knows everything!" Her voice gets higher, carrying around the room.

"But I'm not a senior royal. Why does anyone care about who I date?" My voice is quiet, still flicking through the magazines spread out in front of us.

"Don't be naive, Charlotte. The press doesn't care about that. You're a royal, therefore you are ripe for the picking."

"But we weren't doing anything wrong!" I force myself to meet her gaze. It's punishing. Something I've never felt from her before.

"Did you see the last article?" She pulls one from the back, dropping it on top of the pile.

Another royal abandoning her duties for a Davies brother?

"THEY CAN'T HONESTLY BELIEVE THAT." I push it away from me, unable to look at the horrid news any longer.

"And yet, there is now a pool on the odds of you renouncing your place in the line of succession."

Tears wet my eyes. This can't be happening. "Of course I'm not going to renounce my place. I'm not Ellie."

"I never thought Ellie would, but here we are. It's hard enough keeping the press from releasing photos of James's past, but now I have to worry about talk of another royal leaving. Next thing I know, they'll be calling to abolish the monarchy all together."

"Who is talking about doing that?" Sure, there are people who don't like the monarchy in the modern age, but to abolish the monarchy? It's never been given any real thought.

"The number of scandals since I ascended the throne

reflects poorly on me and upon us all. If the people think I can't control my own family, how will they think I could be a steadfast force for this nation?"

For the first time, I see the worry my aunt carries around. Being Queen isn't easy. Being the fifth in line growing up, it was never a worry for me of actually taking the throne. But with Grandfather dying, Ellie renouncing, and James's past causing him all sorts of problems, the stress she bears breaks through.

"I didn't think who I dated would be that much of a problem."

"Yet you continued to date Pierce behind my back, against my wishes. I won't allow it anymore. You will stop seeing him. I know you take your royal responsibilities seriously and will do the right thing."

I rear back, her words a slap to the face. "You can't be serious. There's no salacious gossip being spread. I still continue to do good work in the name of you and the crown. There has to be another way."

She slaps her hands on the desk, rising before me. It takes everything I have not to flinch away from her. "You will end things at once. You're dismissed."

I don't waste another minute, scurrying from her presence. By the time I escape down the halls, tears are flowing freely.

Pierce and I had the best weekend in Bibury. I thought it was just the two of us, no need to sneak around. But I was wrong. Now that the Queen knows, there's no more sneaking around. The press knows. I'm sure by now, Pierce knows.

My heart is tearing in two at the thought of ending things. There has to be another way. I'm not like Ellie. I have no desire to give up my role as a working royal. I love what I do. I love seeing the people I get to help.

But I love Pierce. I know he loves me. I could feel it in his actions. In the way he held me. Made love to me. I was worried I wouldn't get to keep him. This is why.

How in the world am I supposed to just end things with the one man who has become my entire world?

Shoreditch
INK

Chapter Twenty-Two

PIERCE

I'm staring a hole in the wall. Charlotte texted that she was going to come over so we could talk. I can't imagine what kind of day she's had. My entire family has been blowing up my phone all day, Ellie included, but I've been ignoring them all. The only person I want to talk to should be here by now. I have no idea what's going to happen. I can't imagine the Queen reacted well.

A soft knock at the door has me leaping off the sofa and throwing open the door. I don't waste a moment before pulling Charlotte into my arms. She's stiff. Not her usual relaxed self. Fuck.

"How are you?" I squeeze her tighter to me, not wanting to let go. Her perfume is calming. The first time I've been calm all day.

She pulls out of my arms, taking off her coat and dropping it on the sofa. She doesn't respond to my question. My nerves ratchet up.

"I have to end things with you."

"What?" Her voice is so quiet, I couldn't have heard her correctly. Charlotte looks up at me, tears glazing over her eyes. Her face is bare of any makeup. She's a shell of the vibrant Charlotte she usually is.

"You heard me. It's already causing a scandal."

"But how? How has it come down to that?" I go to her, trying to take her in my arms, but she pulls back.

"Because there are now odds on if I'll leave the royal family. On whether or not I'll follow in Ellie's footsteps."

My brows pull together in confusion. "But you don't want to leave the royal family. Why is it an issue?"

"Because Ellie left. Because they think I'm going to follow suit. That you Davies brothers are bad news for the royal family and will try to overthrow the monarchy!" She throws her hands up in exasperation.

"Can't you tell her that's not the truth?" My heart is beating a rapid pace against my ribs, trying to escape my chest.

"You have to see it from her perspective. She's been rattled by one thing after another since she became Queen. It hasn't been an easy road, and she's trying to control what she can."

"I don't bloody well care! It shouldn't come down to this. She shouldn't get a say if we continue seeing one another. That's fecking insane."

Charlotte winces. I have no idea what's going through her head. She's always been an open book, so easy to read. But for the first time, she's closed off.

"What are you thinking?" I try to find her gaze, but her eyes are moving all over my flat. Like she's seeing it for the last time and trying to memorise it. Fuck. Fuck, fuck, fuck.

This woman. This beautiful, kind, wonderful woman that I've fallen in love with is going to choose the crown over me.

There's no way she could give up the royal life for me. It's not even a possibility. I've seen the way Charlotte lights up when she's talking about her work. She loves it. She was made for it.

The ache in my chest grows. If Charlotte gave up her life for me, she'd regret it. She might be happy for a while, but it would end with her resenting me. And that thought is too much for me to bear.

"There has to be a way around this." Charlotte's words are said more to herself than me.

The hurt in her eyes is evident. But with my next words, it will be a torrent of pain.

"I guess it's as good a time as any to end. Not like we were in love or anything." I'm surprised my voice stays steady. I know the moment the words register because Charlotte's face goes ashen.

"What?" Her voice shakes.

I shrug my shoulders as if this isn't ripping me apart. "We both knew this thing between us wouldn't last. I'm not royal material, and you need someone who is ready to lead by your side."

"You don't believe that." Charlotte presses the heel of her hand to her chest, as if willing her heart not to break.

"There's a reason the Queen didn't want us together. Best to move on with people in our own social standing. It's obvious I could never meet the standards expected to be with a royal."

Charlotte rounds the sofa, stopping in front of me. Her small hands wrap around my forearms. It takes everything inside of me to not pull her into my arms and tell her we can run off together. "Where is this coming from? You can't possibly mean this."

"If you really wanted to be with me, we wouldn't have had to hide our relationship."

"Pierce." Her voice breaks. Tears gather in the corners of her eyes, and fuck me, I can't stand to see her like this.

But it'll be better this way. She can meet someone who the Queen will approve of, and I can live out the rest of my lonely life living in my brother's shadow. "You know I would've shouted our relationship from the top of The Eye if we could have," she implores.

"That's just it." I shake her off, pacing in front of the small window. Londoners are going about their night on the street below, while our world in here is crashing down on us. "If you weren't ashamed of me, we never would have had to hide our relationship."

"You know I was never ashamed of you. Pierce, look at me." Charlotte plants a hand over my heart, stopping my movement. I can't look at her. My eyes will give me away.

"Is what it is, Charlotte. We had fun. Good sex, but that's not enough to stick around, is it?"

Charlotte's gasp has her pulling her hand off me. Looking at her face, I know exactly what heartbreak looks like. Like telling the woman you'd die for that she's nothing more than good sex so she ends up hating you. "That's all this was to you? Good sex?"

I steel myself, going in for the kill. "What man wouldn't like putting his bare dick in a woman's pussy?"

The sting of her slap reverberates through my body. "You bloody bastard! I never want to see you again."

Charlotte spins on her heel, grabbing her coat and taking what's left of my heart with her.

I couldn't keep her, and now, she'll never be mine.

Chapter Twenty-Three

"**M**iss Charlotte. Would you like to play football with us?" The tiny hand tugging me towards the pitch is happy, not a care in the world.

"I would love to. Do you like playing football?" All the students are crowding around me as we make our way outside the school.

"I love it. The boys don't like me playing with them because I'm better than them."

Figures. "Do you hope to play for the national team someday?"

Her baby face is excited. "It's my dream. I want to beat all the boys."

I give her a high five. "I know you can do it!"

"You can play offense with me. You look like a good runner."

I can't help but laugh at her. She'll have a career in coaching if football doesn't work out.

The teacher blows the whistle, and all the students start moving around me. It's not your standard pitch size, but the kids are running around, passing the ball. I try and stay back out of the action, letting the kids have the fun, but I get passed the ball and take off down the pitch. "Shoot it!"

I hit the ball towards the net, and it goes sailing in. "Goal!" All the students converge on me. Hugs and high fives are given as joy takes over. I haven't felt this good since…Bibury. The thought strikes me down as a bone deep ache settles over me. The pain is constant, Pierce's words on a loop playing in my head. I can't turn them off, no matter how hard I try.

"You all did brilliantly! Now let me see you all play and I'll watch." The excitement is palpable on their faces.

"You're quite good with them." The teacher is on the sidelines, watching as the game takes off.

"They make it easy. You have a great group of students here."

"We appreciate all you do for our school. Your support makes all the difference here to be able to achieve our goals."

Another goal is scored, and students run around the pitch in excitement. The excitement of the students is why I love what I do. Seeing how we can support them in achieving their dreams, whatever they may be, is why I could never give up the crown.

It doesn't make the pain of not having Pierce by my side any less. I guess you can't have everything you want.

"ZARA. WHAT ARE YOU DOING HERE?" Zara's at my door, bottle of wine in hand.

"You seem like you need a friend right now." The kindness in her eyes has mine welling up.

"Thank you." I waste no time pulling her in for a hug. It's been a long few days. I've done everything I can to keep myself distracted from the pain that threatens to split me in two. But it's no use.

Every night I come home to my empty apartment at the palace, and it thrusts everything I'm missing in my life into a harsh light. The charity I want to start? In the Queen's hands. Pierce by my side? Think again.

"How are you doing?" Zara follows me into the kitchen, grabbing two glasses and pouring the wine.

"Would you believe me if I said I was right as rain?" I plaster a fake smile on my face. It seems like it's all I can muster lately.

"If you're anything but devastated, I won't believe you. I saw how you talked about Pierce."

"And how is that?" I swirl the wine, not looking at her.

"Like you lost the love of your life." I risk a glance at Zara. Her deep brown eyes are sad. "You look exactly how I felt when I thought I lost James."

"Oh bollocks." Tears leak from my eyes unchecked. I cover my face, trying to hide them, but it's not use.

Zara's arm comes around my shoulders. "It's going to be okay."

"How do you know that?" I bark out, feeling like it will be anything but okay.

"Because it was for James and me. What could he have done that was that bad?"

"All I was to him was a warm pussy to wet his dick." Zara blanches and leans back. "His words, not mine." The anger that was simmering comes back in a rushing tidal wave. "I mean, who says that to someone? How could I have been so stupid to believe that he was in love with me?"

"Based on how he treated you, from what you've told me, it was love." Zara's voice is quieter this time.

"Just because he took me to his family cottage and bought me skates to live out my dream of being a roller girl, doesn't mean he loved me."

"He bought you skates?"

I nod, gulping down my wine. "Doesn't mean he was in love with me."

"Oh, Charlotte." Zara pats my arm. "Don't hate me for saying this, but I saw those pictures in the tabloids." I pierce her with a vicious stare. She throws her hands up in defence. "When your advisors make it their business to know, they tell you. Beside the point. Pierce was in love with you."

I sigh, dropping my head down on my arm. "It's no use. There's no way we could be together even if that were true. The Queen forbids it. You should have seen her face when she saw the papers."

"Honestly? I know she's going to be my mother-in-law, but the woman still scares me. She has this face that you don't want to mess with." I lift my head up as Zara shudders.

"That's exactly the face I got." I throw my hands up in the air. "See! It's useless. I'm going to die alone."

"Well, you will with that attitude." Zara gulps down her wine before rubbing her hands together. "You need a plan to take on the Queen with. I know you have it in you."

"Zara, I love you, but I really *don't* have it in me right now. I just want to be sad. Even sending her my updated charity idea didn't make me happy."

"Why didn't it make you happy? You've been working on that for ages."

"Because Pierce was helping me with the final idea."

"It's still your idea. Your plan." Zara's voice is firm. "I just have a good feeling about it."

"I wish I had your positive attitude right now."

Zara shoves my shoulder. "If I kept up that attitude, I wouldn't soon be marrying the best man I know." The smile that plays on her lips is nothing but love.

I'd hate her if I didn't love her so much. "Zara, I love you, but can you please drop it?"

Zara gives me her teacher face. I know I'm not going to like what comes next.

"Fine. I'll drop it for now, but I won't let you lose the love of your life because of the Queen."

I laugh, watery from the tears still streaming down my face. "You make it sound so easy."

"Oh, I've got a master plan ready to go." She taps her temple like she's a genius.

"And what do you plan on doing?"

"Withholding grandchildren. If you're not happy, then no grandbabies for her."

"And your husband would be okay with this?"

Zara rolls her eyes at me. "How do you think we'll get the Queen on board with our plan?"

Evil genius indeed.

Shoreditch 
INK

Chapter Twenty-Four

PIERCE

"You bloody wanker. You're dating the princess and you didn't tell us?" Liam sounds pissed.

"Were dating," I mumble to myself, pulling my socks up. These last two weeks have been absolutely miserable. I get no relief from my misery. Every person who comes through the shop asks me if I was the guy spotted with Princess Charlotte. At home, everything reminds me of Charlotte. From meals eaten together in my small kitchen to sex in my…well, everywhere. I can't even escape to Bibury, because that reminds me of her too.

"You broke up with the princess?"

I stomp my cleats on the pitch, ready to play. I need the physical activity to calm the constant ache churning in my gut. It's dark, the bitter cold sweeping through London. It matches my mood. Dark, cold, and bitter. "Yes. Now let's play."

"Hold up." Hunter stops me before I get two steps out on the pitch. "You were dating the princess and didn't tell us. What the fuck happened?"

"Christ. Can't you two let this go?" My gaze shifts

between Hunter and Liam. "We dated. Now we're not. End of story."

"You're one of our best mates, Pierce. Based on how you're acting, it's not exactly 'end of story.'"

Fucking intuitive prick. "We never would've worked out. People were against us from the start, so it was better we called things off before anyone caught feelings."

"This is you not catching feelings?" Liam waves his hand over me. "Because, fuck, mate. You look like someone told you Santa isn't real."

That gets a laugh out of me. "What do you mean, Santa isn't real?"

Liam pulls me into a side hug, like only a man can do. "Seriously. Were you happy with her?"

More than I ever admitted to her. Maybe if I grew a pair and told her how I felt, we wouldn't be in this mess. But I saw how she talked about her work. How it lit her up from the inside out. And no matter how much I loved her, I couldn't take her away from that.

"What does it matter now?" I grumble, shoving away from Liam and jogging out onto the pitch.

"What does it matter now?" Liam parrots back to me, still not giving this up. "I've never seen you so cranky before. Shit, were you in love with her?"

That stops me in my tracks. And by the knowing look on his face, he knows it.

"Bloody hell, mate. We need to get her back."

I crack my neck, ready to be done with this. "Why bother? If we couldn't be together before, we can't be together now."

Liam shakes his head, kicking one of the balls over towards me. "Not with that attitude."

"How would you suggest I win her back? It's not like we ended on good terms." I'm humouring him. The look on Charlotte's face when she left is burned into my mind. I won't be able to forget it as long as I live. It was the face of someone who never wanted to see me again. Cutting down the woman I love like that was more brutal that I ever could have imagined.

"We can't rely on your charming personality." I kick the ball back to Liam with more force than necessary. "Can't you just tell her you made a mistake?"

I laugh, for probably the first time in two weeks. "Yes, Liam. If it were that easy, I'd ring up Charlotte, tell her I made a mistake, and all would be forgiven. Christ, no wonder you've never had a girlfriend."

"Just saving all this for that special someone."

Hunter claps him on the back. "Just keep telling yourself that. Now, are you two done? I'm ready to kick some arse tonight."

"LET'S GO GRAB A DRINK. Commiserate our collective loss." We got our arses handed to us tonight. 5-0. It's like we'd never played football before in our lives. Just more bitterness to add to my ever depressing mood.

"Drinks on the moody wanker," Hunter calls out, jogging off the pitch.

"Which one is the moody wanker? We all lost tonight."

"The moodiest of us all. You." Liam tosses his bag over his shoulder, getting ready to leave.

I grab my phone from my bag and see dozens of missed calls from Sean. "Shite."

I dial his number, panic settling over me. Did something happen to Ellie or the baby?

"Where the bloody hell have you been? Ellie's having the baby!" His voice is loud. So loud I have to hold the phone away from my ear.

"Are you serious? It's two weeks early!"

"No shite. Babies come on their own time."

"Where are you? Which hospital?" I start grabbing my stuff, throwing it into my bag.

"St. Stephen's. Get here as fast as you can."

"Is everything all right?" He wouldn't be calling me like this if something was wrong, right?

"It's fine. Just need my brother here." He clicks off, a happy feeling bubbling inside me. I can't stop the smile from spreading across my face.

"Was that Charlotte calling to beg you to take her back?" Liam quirks his eyebrows at me.

"Fuck, let it go, man. I'll be fine."

"You won't be, but whatever you need to believe." His face is dead serious as the words leave his mouth.

"Fuck off. Ellie's having the baby, so I've got to go." I give him a brief hug, excitement at meeting my new niece or nephew coursing through me.

"Shit. You're going to be an uncle? Get outta here, Uncle Pierce. We'll toast to the new little baby." Liam's smile is almost as big as mine.

"Uncle Pierce. That does have a nice ring to it."

I wave to all the guys, running off the pitch. Of all the directions I thought my night would take, meeting my brother's baby wasn't on the list. But now, it's the only thing that's bringing me happiness. I've been a sad sack since Charlotte left, so seeing this new person will be the high-light of my day. Hell, my week.

"SO WHO'S GOING to give you your first tattoo?" Ellie gave birth to a healthy baby boy, Edward, who's now curled up in my arms. "Dad shouldn't be allowed to do it."

"Fuck off, you wanker." This is going to be a fun way to rile up my brother.

"Could you please not talk about tattooing my baby? And maybe lay off the swear words. I don't want his first word being F-U-C-K." Ellie enunciates each letter, driving home her point. Her voice belies her exhaustion. She's tired. She's snuggled next to Sean on the bed, while I hold my new nephew. He's got a full head of brown hair. The tiniest set of fingers peek out over the blanket he's wrapped up tight in.

"It's going to be so easy to tease your dad." Edward is quite possibly the cutest baby I've ever seen. Granted, my experience is limited, and I'm biased.

"I'll be your favourite uncle." His little face screws up, and he lets out a loud cry. "Ouch, kid." Sean walks over, grabbing him from my arms. He's a natural, cuddling him into his neck.

"It's okay if you don't like Uncle Pierce. I didn't like him much when we brought him home."

"I really hope you don't give him another brother." I lean down and drop a kiss on Ellie's head. "I should get going. The shop isn't going to run itself tomorrow."

"I appreciate you helping out while I'm gone." Seeing the way Sean looks at Ellie further shatters the pieces of my heart. What I wouldn't give to be able to have a moment like this with Charlotte. It was hard to see the big picture when we were sneaking around, but it's as if everything became clear the moment she left my apartment.

Charlotte is all I want in life. It would be hard to be in the spotlight. To have people want to be my friend for no other reason than what I could do for them. But it would be okay. Because she's worth it. Charlotte is worth everything I'd be giving up in order to support her in her life's work.

"Pierce, are you okay?" Ellie gives me a despondent look. Shit, I'm not doing a very good job at hiding my feelings lately.

"I'm good. Promise."

Before Ellie can respond, a security officer walks into their private room. I guess being a former royal still has some privileges.

My stomach drops to the floor. Would Charlotte come to the hospital? Whatever clarity I just had goes into hiding. I'm not ready to face her yet. Would she even want to see me?

Panic runs wild as the Queen enters the suite Ellie is staying in.

"Mum! What are you doing here?"

"Isn't this what normal mums do?" Her smile is easy as she enters the room. She's wearing jeans and a jumper under her coat. I don't think I've ever seen the Queen so dressed down. But it is well past two in the morning.

"Would you like to hold him?" Sean's voice is steady as he sets the small baby in her arms, not even awaiting an answer.

"He's beautiful. Have you decided on a name yet?"

"Edward." Ellie's eyes well up, mirroring her mum's.

"You'll have a lot to live up to, little one."

With the Queen here now, it feels like I'm intruding on

a family moment. But the security officers are blocking the door. Fuck. All I want to do now is leave.

"Mum. You remember Pierce, Sean's brother?" Ellie's words are soft. I love her for trying to bring me into the mix, but all it does is remind me what I don't have. That Charlotte isn't here with me. That both of Edward's godparents weren't here to welcome him into the world.

"Yes. Pleasure to see you. I hope you're doing well." She gives me a small nod. One that sets me off.

"I'd be doing much better if Charlotte were here." The Queen's eyes are hard as she turns to me. She's not a woman to be messed with. But I don't care. Because of her, I lost the love of my life. I pushed her away because she couldn't give up her life's work.

"Pierce. Now is not the time." Sean's voice is stern.

"I don't bloody well care. Because of her, Charlotte and I aren't together anymore. It's not fair that you two get to be together and we can't."

"And this little outburst of yours tells me all I need to know." The Queen turns back to the baby in her arms.

"Mum. That's not fair." Ellie's voice is hard as the tension in the room thickens.

"Excuse me if I'm having a hard time containing my emotions. I only lost the love of my life." I scrub a hand down my face. Christ, I've made this all about me. "I need to go. I'm sorry. Congrats, you two. I can't wait to come over and see him." I drop a kiss on Ellie's cheek, but a voice stops me. One I wasn't expecting.

"Come see me at the palace on Tuesday promptly at noon. You and I need to have a discussion." This time, the Queen's eyes aren't as hard.

Bloody hell, they don't still behead people, do they?

Shoreditch
INK

Chapter Twenty-Five

PIERCE

"Anyone home?" I call out, pushing open Ellie and Sean's front door. They brought Edward home from the hospital last night, and I was already itching to see him. That and sitting at home by myself waiting to meet the Queen has me antsy.

"Are you insane?" Sean whisper-yells. "What if Edward was sleeping? You could've woken him up."

"Was he asleep?"

"Well, no. But you just can't come yelling into the house anymore."

I raise my hands in defence. "Sorry. Lesson learned. Where is the little bugger?"

"Is that your Uncle Pierce I hear?" Ellie walks out from the kitchen, baby in her arms. Her pink hair is pulled up in a messy bun and her eyes are tired. But I've never seen her happier.

"Wanted to see my nephew." His eyes are wide as Ellie moves the tight bundle into my arms.

"Can you at least call before you come over?" Sean's voice tries to be annoyed, but it's anything but.

"Don't listen to your brother. Anytime you want to come over is fine. Just be warned, you might not see me because I might be napping."

"That's just fine. I can hang out with my new buddy," I coo. Big blue eyes meet mine. Christ, if this isn't the cutest kid in the world.

"Good to know you don't need to see us."

I look up, Sean now wrapped around Ellie. "Tough shit. You'll have to get used to people wanting to see Edward and not you."

"Again, with the swearing. I would like it if our son's first words were mama or dada and not fuck or shit."

"Pink. How dare you cuss in front of Edward." I cover his little head, shifting him away from her. "Sorry, Edward. I'll make sure no one uses such foul language around you."

Ellie shakes her head. "Unbelievable."

A knock at the door has Ellie leaving us behind.

"Oh, Charlotte. I forgot you were coming."

My heart stalls in my chest. Charlotte's here? Sean gives me the same panicked look that is currently pulsing through my veins.

Charlotte and Ellie appear from the entryway, and Charlotte stops cold.

"Sorry, I didn't realise you had company. I'll come back later."

"Charlotte, wait." My voice is thick. All I want to do is talk to her, but I have no idea where to start.

Charlotte is out the door before I can get in another word. "Let me go talk to her. I'll see you guys later." I pass Edward over to Sean and run after Charlotte. She's halfway in the car before I can get to her.

"Please don't go," I plead. "Charlotte. We need to talk. Please."

I don't know where this courage is coming from, but

I'm ready to tell her everything. That I love her. That I didn't mean a single word I said. That I broke my own heart as much as hers when she left my apartment that day.

"I can't be here, Pierce. Please. Just let me go." The pain in her voice cracks me in two. My already shattered heart breaks even more.

"No. You stay and visit. Meet your godson."

Her brown eyes are dull and lifeless when she looks up at me. Her face is devoid of any makeup, her usually dark red lips natural.

"I can't stay if you're here."

"I'm going. But Charlotte?" Wetness hangs on her eyelashes as she peers up at me. "We need to talk. Maybe not now, but later. This can't be the end for us."

She steels her spine, straightening as she steps back out of the car. "No. The end for us was when you crushed my heart in your flat." She spins on her heel and walks back into Ellie and Sean's. The slam of the door reverberates through me, rattling all the broken pieces. Christ, I don't know if she'll take me back. Even getting the Queen's approval won't mean anything if she can't even look at me.

What have I done?

Charlotte

"ARE YOU OKAY?" Ellie's voice is quiet as we sit on the sofa. Baby Edward looks just like Pierce. His bright blue eyes. Full head of dark hair. Looking at him makes me ache.

"No." I rub a finger over Edward's chubby cheeks. He's staring at me with wide eyes, like he isn't sure who I am.

"Don't you even want to hear him out?" Ellie moves closer, wrapping an arm around me.

"How can I? I can't even be in the same room as him without wanting to cry." I bite down on my quivering lips. Whenever I've had a quiet moment these last two weeks, tears flood my eyes. I'm sick of crying over Pierce. I loved him, but he clearly didn't love me. I should be able to move past that. But my heart won't let me.

"Oh, sweetheart." Ellie smooths a hand over my cheek. Such a mothering gesture. "I know he didn't mean those words."

I called Ellie in tears when I left Pierce's flat. She tried to talk through it with me, but I was too distraught. My heart has never been broken like that. Crushed. Shattered.

"You didn't see his face." Edward starts to fuss, so I bring him to my shoulder, rubbing his back.

"But I've seen him almost every day since." I love Ellie for not picking sides. Hard to when she's with his brother. "That's not the look of a man who isn't in love."

"Then why did he tell me I was nothing more than a p-u-s-s-y for his d-i-c-k?"

Ellie tries to contain her laugh but can't. "I know you're in pain, but thank you for not cussing in front of my sweet boy."

A smile pulls on my lips. "I try."

"But Charlotte. I don't know why he said that, but it's the furthest thing from the truth."

"And how do you know that?" I rest my head on Edward's. At least he'll never turn on me.

"Because he looks at you the way Sean looks at me."

I suck in a breath. I want someone to look at me the way Sean looks at Ellie. Like I am the centre of his world. That he wouldn't know what to do if I wasn't in his life.

"He can't look at me like that." I shake my head. It's impossible. "I saw the last look he gave me. Not possible."

"Then you're seeing what you want to see. He went toe to toe with Mum the other night."

"What?" No one in their right mind would want to face the Queen. I'm a blood relative, and even I can't push back.

"But you're right." Ellie waves off my earlier comments. "He doesn't love you. He's just taking on Mum for the sake of it."

Edward starts crying, and Ellie takes him from my arms. "I guess you'll just forever wonder why Pierce is taking on the Queen for you."

Why on earth would Pierce talk to Aunt Katherine? He told me he didn't love me. But the man outside looked as broken as I feel. Pierce knew the position I was in. Him or the crown. Did he fall on his sword for me?

That night has been playing like a bad movie through my head nonstop. But Ellie's words have me seeing it in a new light. Did Pierce break up with me so I wouldn't give up my life?

Confusion swirls in my head. If only I knew which way was up and how to move forward.

Because right now, it feels like the only way forward is with Pierce.

And I'm not quite sure I'm there yet.

Shoreditch
INK

Chapter Twenty-Six

PIERCE

"Damn. You do great work. I should've covered this old piece up years ago."

The man is admiring the piece I just finished. It's some of my best work. "Thanks. Need the aftercare instructions, or you know them by now?"

"Nah. I know them." I wipe off the oozing ink, taking another minute to look at my latest piece. "Thanks again." I pull my gloves off with a snap, taking the cash from his hand.

"Hopefully you won't have any need to cover this one up in the future."

He shakes his head. "Not a chance in hell."

"Cheers." I wave him off, going about clearing my station.

"He seemed quite happy." Sean's head pops over the wall.

"What are you doing here? Shouldn't you be at home with Ellie and the baby?"

A loved-up look washes over his face. My chest aches at the thought of never getting that feeling again with Charlotte. The look of pure anguish on her face yesterday gutted me. I couldn't let her give up her work, but hopefully, after my talk with the Queen tomorrow, we might get that back.

"Wanted to talk to you about something." He nods his head towards the back, and I follow him.

"What's up?" He closes the door behind me before sitting behind his desk.

"I wanted to talk to you about becoming a partner in the shop."

Shock doesn't even begin to describe what I'm feeling. "A partner?"

"Why do you sound so surprised?" Sean leans back in his chair, grabbing a bottle of gin and pouring two glasses.

"I just never thought you thought that highly of my work." I sip the drink, wincing through the burn.

"Why the fuck would I keep you here if I didn't?"

"Because I'm your brother."

Sean stands, coming around to where I'm sitting. "I'm still a businessman. If you sucked, I wouldn't string you along." I eye the clear liquid, swirling it in the glass. "You're one of the best cover-up artists in the city, and I want to make you a partner. Expand on the business."

"You really want to do that with me?"

"Of course I do. Do you know how many people come in here and ask for you?"

My eyes fly up to meet his. "Are you fucking with me? Everyone always comes in here asking for you."

Sean shakes his head, sitting in the empty chair next to me. "I guess I don't do a good enough job telling you how good you're doing. I have people coming in here all the time asking for you. It's almost giving me a complex."

"Welcome to my life," I mumble to myself.

"Pierce." Sean claps me on the shoulder, shifting my

gaze back to him. "I'm sorry that I haven't told you how good you are and made you question your work. You're one of the best tattoo artists I've ever worked with, and I set the bar pretty high. I wouldn't be asking you to do this if I wasn't serious."

"You'd really want me to be your partner?"

"Fuck, yes. There's nothing that would make me happier. Is it what you want?"

"I mean, yeah." My voice is quiet, not quite conveying how I feel.

"Wow, way to sell me that you want to be here." Sean's voice is easy.

I run a hand down my scruffy face. I haven't bothered to shave the last few days. "Sorry. I just can't get Charlotte out of my head."

"Do you think meeting with the Queen tomorrow will help?"

"Fuck, I don't know." I stand, pacing the room. "I have to try though. All I want is to be with Charlotte, but I can't let her give up her work. It lights her up."

"Even if you get approval, it won't be easy. People still follow Ellie around, and I wish I could do more to protect her, but I can't. You'll never get an ounce of privacy again. Is that really what you want?"

"Yes." I answer without hesitation.

Sean smirks. The bastard. "Then that's what you need to tell the Queen. You're not some bloke off the street." His smile widens. "You're a partner in a thriving business, and anyone would be lucky to have you as a member of their family."

Hope blooms in my chest for the first time in what feels like ages. "I don't think I've ever gotten quite the pep talk from you. Maybe I need to be mopey more often."

Sean sets his drink down, crossing his ankles. "I hate

seeing you like this, but I promise it'll be okay. I have a feeling things are going to fall into place for you. Here and with Charlotte."

"Well, at least I know I'll always have my work."

"Does that mean you'll be a partner with me?"

I give Sean a big smile. "Someone has to keep you in line."

The faith and trust my brother is putting in me is huge. We're on the same playing field. All this time I've been focusing on why his work is better than mine, why I play second fiddle to him, but I was wrong. We both shine in our own ways. His words mean more to me than he'll ever know. And I can't wait to see where this takes us.

Sean stands, pulling me in for a hug. "I love you, Pierce. I know things will work out with Charlotte. They did for me and Ellie."

I just pray those words are true.

Shoreditch
INK

Chapter Twenty-Seven

PIERCE

I don't think I've ever been so nervous in my entire life. Sure, I was nervous when I did my first tattoo, but nothing compares to this. I apologised profusely to Ellie for making such a show when Edward was born. But she said she understood. She knows the pain I was in from losing Charlotte.

But now, I'm sitting in the Queen's office, waiting for her to arrive. I'm so nervous I could puke.

"Mr. Davies? Her Majesty will see you now." I stand, buttoning my jacket, as I'm shown into the fanciest room I've ever seen. Portraits older than generations of my ancestors hang on the walls. Heavy purple drapes block the grey London skies from piercing through. A chandelier hangs overhead. I'm afraid if I touch anything, it might break.

"Pierce. Thank you for joining me today."

I bow. Her presence is more overwhelming in here than I thought. I'm surprised I haven't passed out yet. "The pleasure is mine, Your Majesty." At least Mum would be proud of my manners. As much as I want to tell the Queen off again, I know it's not in my best interest.

"I'm sure you're wondering why I called you here today."

I give her a tight smile. "First let me apologise to you for my outburst at the hospital. It was inappropriate. I wasn't in a good place at the time, and it wasn't right to do that at such a happy moment."

She sighs, shaking her head. "I was hoping I could apologise to you."

Shock colours my face. "Apologise to me?"

She gives me a stiff nod. "I'm afraid I was wrong about you, Pierce."

"Wrong how?" My palms are starting to sweat under her watchful eye.

"As you know, it's been a hard year. With Ellie renouncing her place in line to the throne, and James and Zara's scandal, it's been hard to lead the country as I want to."

"Is that why you've been so hard on Charlotte?" I blurt out. Shit. I want to take the words back as soon as I say them.

She gives me a warm smile, one that sets me at ease. "You're astute, Pierce. I'm afraid when I saw the photos of you and Charlotte together, I thought I'd have another Ellie situation on my hands."

"Even though Charlotte loves what she does and wants to contribute more, you thought I was going to make her give up her place?" Bitterness laces my tone. Nice to know how they really feel about you.

"And that is why I'm apologising. A Queen can admit when she's wrong."

"And that's it? I go back to my life and be a miserable sod because I can't have Charlotte?"

The Queen stands, coming around her desk. "I'm going to be frank with you, Pierce. This life is hard. A camera is shoved in your face daily. Any wrong move and it's fodder for the entire world. I'm shocked you two weren't discovered before. Is this really how you see your future?"

"Yes," I answer without hesitation. "I know what Charlotte's life is like. I know what Ellie still goes through. I know people probably take one look at me and make a snap judgment on what I'm like, but I want this. I want to support Charlotte on the hard days and keep her moving forward in the work she does. I want to be with Charlotte more than I ever thought possible. I love her."

"And you're ready to give up your privacy? Stand by Charlotte's side while she serves her country?"

I nod my head. "If you're trying to scare me away, it won't work."

She crosses her arms, giving me a knowing look. "And is that why you broke up with Charlotte in the first place?"

"How in the world do you know about that?"

"It doesn't matter."

"I broke up with her because I wasn't going to make her give up everything she loves just for me. She would resent me if she had to."

"That's very noble of you." The Queen goes back around her desk and scribbles something on a piece of paper, before dropping it in a file and handing it to me. "Meet Charlotte at this address at seven sharp tonight. Don't be late."

I stand, taking the folder. "What, that's it?"

"I think you've proven that you know what you're getting yourself into. Unless you have something else to say?" She raises a perfectly manicured brow at me.

"Thank you for your time." I bow, trying not to run out of her office. I don't want to test her patience any further.

Did she really just give me permission to date Charlotte? Hope blooms in my chest.

I only hope Charlotte will hear me out.

Charlotte

SNOW SWIRLS around me as I step out of the car and head into the restaurant. I didn't want to come tonight. It's taken all my energy to make it through each day this last week, so meeting someone at the Queen's request isn't my first idea of a good night. I wanted to curl up and eat my weight in ice cream. But no. When the Queen wants something, you're at her every whim.

"Ahh, Princess Charlotte. It's a pleasure to have you here this evening. Your party is awaiting your arrival." The hostess curtsies to me before leading me through the dimly lit restaurant. Dark cherry wood lines the walls, casting long shadows from the old lights hanging overhead. "Here you are." She gestures towards the booth in front of me and I stop.

All the breath leaves my lungs as Pierce stands in front of me. If my feet weren't stuck to the ground, I'd be running out of here right now.

"I'm sure you're wondering why I'm here." I hate that his voice washes over me, causing heat to erupt in my veins. That his bright blue eyes are pleading with me to sit down. The hostess's eyes are flitting back and forth between the two of us. Not wanting to cause a scene, I take a seat, as Pierce drops down across from me.

"How have you been?" His voice is quiet as he takes me in. He's not the same Pierce I'm used to seeing. Purple shadows hang under his eyes. His smile isn't happy like it usually is.

"Oh, I don't know. Just trying to figure out why I make such terrible life choices. Why men don't want to stick around."

Pierce winces. I should feel bad, but I don't. Not after he made love to me and then ripped my heart out.

"If you let me—"

"Good evening. Can I start you off with something to drink?" comes a cheery voice as our server interrupts him.

"I'll take a whisky neat." My voice is curt, my eyes not leaving Pierce as he orders a scotch.

He holds my gaze, not speaking until our drinks are dropped off. The waiter seems to be ready to take our order, but one look at my face and he scurries off. I'm not in the mood for playing games tonight. I take a steadying gulp of my drink before focusing on Pierce.

"Why are you here tonight?"

"No one told you?" Confusion mars his handsome face.

"I was given explicit instructions to be here at seven sharp." By the Queen. Why would she want me to meet Pierce here?

"I met with the Queen today." His voice is quiet, as if he's unsure if the ground he's treading on is safe.

"You what?" Shock colours my features. "How did you get a meeting with her?"

He takes a sip of his drink, the liquid glistening on his lips. Oh, how I've missed kissing those lips. The way they'd make me feel. Bring me pleasure. Make me feel loved.

"I sort of yelled at her at the hospital, and then she told me to meet her at the palace."

This time, I can't keep my shock to myself as a laugh bubbles out of me. "You yelled at her? Not many people can get away with something like that."

Pierce shrugs. "I must've caught her at a good moment. She had come to the hospital to visit the baby."

"And what did you discuss with her?" My nerves are frayed. The longer I sit here, the more I want to be swept up into this man's arms. But he rejected me. In the worst way. And now all I want to do is go home and let out all these emotions that are coiling up inside of me.

"How I want to be with you."

I roll my eyes, finishing off my drink. "Right. Why would you want to be with me when I'm nothing more than a nice pussy?" I throw his words at him. He at least looks ashamed. Good. Now he knows a tenth of what I'm feeling.

"You know that wasn't true. How could you even begin to think that?"

"It's not like you ever told me you loved me." I'm staring at my glass. I can't look at him as tears well up in my eyes. I don't want to cry over this man anymore, but it's hard not to.

Pierce is at my side, sliding into my side of the booth. "Look at me, Charlotte."

I close my eyes, gathering the strength to make it through this conversation. When my gaze meets his, those eyes I love so much are heavy. Weighed down with emotion.

"I didn't mean a word of what I said to you. You had to know that as much as it broke your heart that day, it decimated mine."

"Then why would you say such a horrid thing?" My voice wavers.

Pierce's warm hands cup my cheeks, keeping my eyes on his face. "Because I couldn't make you choose. Me or the crown. If I made you choose me, you'd resent me for making you give up your life. You love what you do. I couldn't be the reason you walked away from it."

Pierce thumbs away a tear that falls. "Why didn't you just tell me that?"

He drops his forehead to mine. "Because she was making you choose. She was against us from the start, and no matter what we did, she wasn't going to support us."

I pull back, clasping my hands on his wrists. His pulse is beating a rapid tattoo under my fingertips. "And why is she going to support us now?"

"She is no longer convinced that I will be a bad influence on you." A skeptical laugh leaves my lips. Pierce smiles down on me. "She thought you would follow in Ellie's footsteps and renounce your royal title."

I shake my head, disbelief taking over. "I don't know why everyone thinks I can't make up my own mind. I'm not Ellie. Sean didn't convince her to give up the crown. She was unhappy. What do I have to do to prove I'm not going anywhere?"

"I also told Queen Katherine how I know what your life is like and how people will always make snap judgments about me. About how I always want to be with you. I know I'm giving up my privacy, but I want to be by your side while you serve this country."

"What?" My voice is quiet. My eyes rake over his face, trying to find doubt there. But there is none. His face is strong.

"Charlotte, I love you. I love you more than I ever thought possible. You are brilliant at what you do. I could never take you away from the people that need you. I guess the Queen just needed to hear it from me that I would support you in everything you do."

"What are you saying?"

Pierce licks his lips, threading his fingers through the hair at my neck. My heartbeat is erratic, waiting with bated breath for what he says next.

"I also told the Queen how I knew what I was getting myself into. That I'm prepared to support you for the rest of my life. How you need a partner to keep you moving forward on the hard days. Someone willing to live a very public life in order to be a part of your life."

I can't control the tears now. "You said that to her?"

He nods, his tongue darting out to lick his bottom lip. "I did."

I shake my head. "But I'm not worth all of that. The paparazzi following your every move. Nothing about your life will be private. You have to know that."

"You're wrong." Pierce's lips ghost over my cheek, my jaw. They find the shell of my ear. "You are worth it. More than you'll ever know. My life would be incomplete without you. When you walked out of my flat that day, you took my heart with you. You own me, Charlotte. Completely. No one else can compare to you. You're it for me."

I bury my head in his shoulder, hiccuping over the tears. No one has ever said anything like this to me. Made me feel so treasured. So valued.

"I can't believe you went toe to toe with the Queen." I wrap my arms around his waist, needing to feel him. I can't believe I'm here, listening to the words I've been aching to hear from him.

"After seeing Ellie and Sean with Edward, there was no doubt in my mind that I had to fight for you. I would've gone to the palace every day until she listened to me."

I drop a kiss on Pierce's neck before pulling back. His eyes are glassy. "You know you probably would've been arrested for harassing the Queen?"

He lifts a shoulder, as if it's no big deal. "She would've known I was serious."

"You're ready to walk into this chaotic life and be with me? Never having an iota of privacy again?" My head still doesn't believe it. My heart? His words are mending it, stitch for stitch, word by word.

"Love, I'd do anything for you. You and me. That's all I need in life."

I trace my fingers over his face, memorising every detail. I never thought I'd find the kind of love like my cousins have. To feel a love so fierce for someone else, that some days it hurts to breathe. But I've found that with Pierce.

"I love you, Pierce. So much. You broke my heart, but I knew I couldn't be happy without you. Seeing baby Edward reminded me so much of you and it gutted me, thinking we could never have that." A watery smile is painted on my face as Pierce claims my lips.

I lean into him, my tongue tangling with his. I don't hide the groan that escapes. I don't care that we're in the middle of a restaurant. I thought kisses like this were gone when Pierce walked away. But feeling the hunger and passion behind his kiss makes need coil throughout my body.

"That's not the only news I come bearing tonight." Pierce pulls back, his thumbs stroking my cheeks. Nothing but love shines out of his eyes.

"What more could I need?"

"How about a new charity to run with your boyfriend?"

"Mm, I like the sound of that."

"Running a charity?" His voice is playful.

"No, my boyfriend. Doesn't seem to fit with how much I love you."

Pierce wraps an arm around my shoulder as we sink into the booth. The scent of his cologne wafts over me. I forgot how calming it was.

"Don't you want to know about the charity?" His voice is a whisper in my hair. He passes a folder I didn't notice on the table over to me.

"I'm sure it's something the Queen is dumping on me because no one else wants to do it." I'm more than a little skeptical of her motivations, even if she sent me to Pierce here tonight.

"What if it has to do with the women's foundation you've been wanting to start?" I pull back out of his arms, my mouth gaping open in shock.

"You mean…are you serious?" I plant my hands on his chest, keeping him at arm's length. "This would be a really mean joke if you aren't serious."

He shakes his head, pulling me back to him. "I'm serious. I know how badly you want this, and I'm invested in it. I want to see this succeed. If you'll have me." I flip open the folder and my proposal, the one I worked on with Pierce, has notes from the Queen on advisors who can help make it work. I can't believe it.

Everything about this night is surreal. I didn't expect to see Pierce here. I didn't expect to get my charity that I've been fighting for. Everything is falling into place.

"I can't believe you got her to change her mind on this." Pierce's wide smile is bright. Butterflies break out in my stomach. "We really get to do this?"

"I had nothing to do with it. It was all you, love."

"I don't know what magical powers you have, but you've somehow pulled the Queen under your spell. I might just have to keep you around." I pull him towards me, taking another kiss. Needing to feel his lips under mine. To know that this moment is real. That I'm not dreaming.

Pierce's lips are soft as they move against mine. I could sit here in this dark restaurant all night if it means I get to stay here with Pierce. I don't want him out of my sight.

"Excuse me." Our server clears his throat. "Can I get you an appetizer to start your meal?"

"Just the cheque." Pierce doesn't look away from me. He drops his mouth to my ear. "I'm ready to take you home and show you just how much I love you."

I shake my head. "My home. I want you to see where we'll be living."

Pierce lifts an eyebrow at me. "Where we'll be living? Pretty presumptuous of you to assume I'll be moving in."

"I have big plans for you, Pierce. I don't want to waste another day without you. I want to marry you and have lots of babies."

"Little princes and princesses running around? Sounds pretty good to me."

"Thought so. Now, take me home and show me just how much you love me."

Pierce drops some pounds on the table, not bothering with the cheque. He pulls me up, my hands colliding with the muscle in his chest. "Your wish is my command, princess."

Chapter Twenty-Eight

The door hasn't shut behind me before Pierce is attacking my lips with his. It's all teeth and tongues. His lips soothe away the sting of the words he said that I haven't been able to get out of my head. But seeing him tonight, the look of love on his face, I know he is it for me.

"Fuck, I've missed you, Charlotte." Pierce picks me up, wrapping me in his arms. His hard length presses into my core. Tears prickle his eyes. "I thought I'd never get to see you again."

"You were doing what you thought was right." My thumb smooths the furrowed line between his brows away. "But it's you and me now. This will be our life." I look around the grand halls of the palace I call home.

Pierce's smile is blinding. "I can't fucking wait." His lips crash down on mine. I wrap my arms around him, holding him as close as possible to me. My nails claw down his chest, fumbling to release him of his shirt.

Giving up, I rip the material away. One button pings off. The rest haven't moved. "Huh. I always thought that would work."

"I'm glad you're so eager, but I want you laid out beneath me. Bedroom?" Pierce's voice is playful. I drop my legs, leading him towards my oversized room. His eyes don't leave me. They don't take in the grand staircase. Or the paintings on the stairs that are centuries old. Family history bearing down on us.

I grab Pierce's hand and lead him to the bed. Sitting on the edge, I work his belt buckle free. I run my hands over the obvious bulge in his pants.

"If you keep doing that, I'm going to come in my pants, and we can't have that." Pierce pushes me back onto the bed. His weight settles over me as his lips blaze a trail of hot kisses down my neck.

I'm a writhing mess beneath him, wanting more, but not wanting his lips to leave mine. Pierce links our hands, stretching them over my head.

"I'm going to strip you bare and feast on you. All I've dreamed about is getting to taste you again." The heat in his eyes has my release barrelling through me. My need to come has never been so high.

"What are you waiting for?"

A smirk dances across Pierce's face. His fingers work their way down my body. Unbuttoning my slacks, the snick of the zipper echoes through the quiet room. I lift my hips, giving him better access to pull them down. He throws them behind me before grasping my ankles and pulling me towards the edge of the bed.

"Looks like someone is ready for me." His lips ghost over the tender flesh of my inner thigh. My thong is wet with need. Pierce is slow with his lips, grazing them over my flesh. Nipping and sucking everywhere but where I really want him.

"You are such a tease." I roll my hips, trying to get him to my aching core.

"Is this where you want me?" His finger trails down my thong before he swipes it to the side.

"God, yes!" I shout.

"I should make you beg." His voice is heated.

"Please, Pierce. Please put your mouth on me." I tilt my head up, his grin downright evil.

"I don't know. It doesn't sound like you're desperate enough." He pushes my shirt up and over my head. Those plump, sinful lips move down my arms. Over the swell of my breasts. Down my belly. He nips at my hip.

"Oh my God. If you don't fuck me, I'm going to die."

"Well, we wouldn't want that, now would we?" His finger slides under the poor excuse for underwear and tears it from my body. "Fuck. You're soaked."

"I need you." No sooner do the words escape than Pierce sucks my clit into his mouth. A deep groan bursts from my lips. My skin is vibrating with need as Pierce laves me with his tongue. He thrusts two fingers inside my pussy, and I'm practically coming apart at the seams.

"Pierce! Don't stop." I thread my fingers through his hair, keeping his mouth on me. The pressure is building, racing down my spine, like a cannon ready to go off.

"Are you ready to come for me, love? I want to feel you come on my tongue and fingers."

His words pull my orgasm from me. Pleasure washes over me as I arch into Pierce's touch. His fingers continue their ministrations through my release. The pressure in my belly eases, a happiness settling over me. I've entered a state of pure bliss.

"You still with me, love?" Pierce kisses his way up my body, his tongue flicking over my hard nipples.

I peek one eye open. His lips are wet with my release, his hair mussed from my hands. "Barely."

"Think you can handle more?" His hand splays over my stomach.

I sit up, moving over him. "If I don't have you buried inside me tonight, I might combust."

Pierce kisses me. Long, languid strokes. I forgot how good kissing him was. "I just got you back. I can't have you combusting on me."

I push Pierce back on the bed, pulling his briefs down his legs. His hard cock springs free. Licking my lips, anticipation builds at the thought of having him inside me.

I grip the base of his cock, giving the vein underneath a long lick. His hips buck off the bed, as I suck his tip into my mouth. "Fuck, Charlotte." His hands wrap around my hair, pulling it away from my face.

Precum leaks onto my tongue, driving my own pleasure higher. "If you keep doing that, love, I'm going to come down your throat, and that's not what I want tonight." I pull off him, wiping my lips.

Pierce's eyes are glazed over as he takes me in. He looks small in my bed. I love having him here in my space. He looks so at ease, so natural, that it makes my heart swell.

Pierce pulls me over him before flipping us to the centre of the bed. The look in his eyes is nothing but love. I can't believe how lucky I am to get to be with this man. To not have to hide our relationship any longer.

Pierce reaches for his jeans, pulling out a condom. "Just in case?"

I nod. "You're in the good graces of the Queen now. Can't have an unplanned pregnancy giving you the boot."

Pierce sheathes himself before sliding inside of me. Wrapping my arms and legs around him, I pull him close to me. Running my fingers through his hair, I stare up into his eyes as he moves inside me.

"God, I've missed you," he whispers against my lips, as he continues moving. Long, slow thrusts.

My heart is so full in this moment, that I get to be with the man of my dreams. A single tear slips out, as Pierce kisses it away.

"You okay, love?"

"As long as I'm with you, I'll be okay." The orgasm that rolls through me is quiet, but powerful. It's how it always is with Pierce.

He drops his forehead to mine as he groans through his own release.

"Promise me it'll never stop being like this?" I whisper against his lips.

"Never."

Pierce pulls out, taking care of the condom before wrapping me in his arms. I could stay like this forever. But my stomach seems to have other ideas.

"Hungry?" Pierce asks, my belly growling again.

I pull Pierce's T-shirt on to cover myself. "Come with me. I've got a little surprise for you."

Pierce smirks, pulling on his briefs. "Didn't you already have something sweet?"

"Aren't you funny." I wrap my arms around his bare chest, his muscles flexing under my fingertips. I drop a kiss over his heart, before threading my fingers through his.

"Are you going to give me a tour?" Our footsteps are quiet as we head down towards the small kitchen I use most days.

"You'll get a tour another time." I grin at him over my shoulder. The soft lights of the apartment are reflected in his eyes. Pierce pulls me back, his chest colliding with my back.

"I like the sound of that." His lips find my neck.

"The sound of what?" Butterflies threaten to burst in me at the slightest touch of his lips on me.

Cupping my chin, Pierce turns my gaze to him. "Next time."

My heart threatens to burst from my chest. God, I love this man.

I lead the way towards the kitchen, turning on a small overhead light. "Sit."

"What's the surprise?" Pierce stretches out in the booth by the window. His abs ripple under the soft light. Long legs stick out from under the table. I don't think I'll ever get used to seeing him here in my space. I grab the small bag and hide it behind my back as I saunter over to Pierce.

"Can you guess?" A sly smile spreads across my face.

"Twenty questions?"

I laugh. "Only twenty."

"Can we make this strip twenty questions? Each question I get wrong you lose an article of clothing?"

I smack his chest. "I'm only wearing a shirt. You'd ask if I had an alien behind my back if it meant you could see my tits."

Pierce's eyes grow dark. "They are very nice tits." He squeezes them together, and it takes everything I have to remember why I came down here.

"Slow down. You don't get these"—I wave in front of my chest—"until you guess what I have."

Pierce snarls at me. "You really don't play fair."

"No." I kiss the corner of his mouth. "Now, start guessing."

"Is it an alien?"

I pinch his side. "You little shite."

"Fine." His hands snake under my shirt, his thumbs rubbing soothing circles at the base of my spine. "Is it chocolate?"

I shake my head, dropping a kiss on his lips. "No."

"Do I get a kiss every time I get one wrong?"

"No, because then you'd never actually give me a real answer."

Pierce leans farther into me, pulling me under his spell. Next thing I know, the bag is ripped from my hands, and I'm sprawled out on the table under him.

"Marshmallows?"

I can't help the giggle that bursts forth. "I haven't been able to stop eating them since we came home from Bibury. And when you…" I can't finish my thought. We're together now. I never want to think of being without him. "Those and wine are all I've been eating the last week. I've been a sodding mess. But marshmallows made it better."

Pierce drops the bag, caging me in under him. "Am I allowed to make it better?"

My fingers rake through the scruff on his jaw. "You've already made it better."

"So these are just the icing on the cake?"

I nod, biting my lip. Pierce takes one, holding it out to me. I sink my teeth into the sugary goodness. Instead of eating the other half, his lips graze mine. His tongue licks the seam of my lips and I open to him.

"Fuck, you taste amazing." His voice is a growl.

"I'm pretty sure that's the marshmallow."

I sit up, pushing Pierce back into the bench. He pops the other half in his mouth, smiling at me.

"You know, this is pretty great," I say with a grin.

"What is?" He grabs one from the bag, and I steal it from him, shoving the whole thing in my mouth.

"Sitting here in my kitchen. Eating marshmallows with you."

Pierce runs his hands up my bare thighs, settling on my

hips. "If this is all you need, I'll promise to always bring home marshmallows."

"Yeah?"

"If it'd make you happy, I'd buy you an entire factory of marshmallows. I never want to see you sad."

"Well that's impossible. No one can ever be that happy."

Pierce pulls me down into his lap, wrapping his arms around me. "As long as I have you, I'll have everything I need in life."

"And as long as I have marshmallows and you, I'll have everything I need in life."

Pierce smiles. "Sounds like a damn good life to me."

Epilogue

CHARLOTTE - ONE YEAR LATER

"Are you nervous?" I smooth the lapels of the suit Pierce is wearing. I love him in anything, but he wears a suit well.

"Love, I think you're more nervous than I am." He grabs my hand, kissing my engagement ring. The pink sapphire set in a burst of diamonds on a rose gold band is my favourite. Pierce picked the perfect ring for me.

"It's going to be a long few days, and I just want to get them over with."

He tips my chin up to look him in the eye. "You want to get our wedding day over with?"

I sigh, wrapping my arms around him. "I don't care about some big wedding. I just want to be married to you. To get to live together and start our life here."

After our engagement, the Queen gifted us a cottage on the grounds of Windsor Castle. We wasted no time making it our own, even though Pierce won't officially live here until after the wedding. It's been lonely without him here.

"You know what I'm looking forward to?" His lips kiss down my jaw.

"What's that?" I close my eyes, relishing his touch.

"The honeymoon."

A laugh escapes my lips. "Of course you are."

We're leaving for the Maldives the morning after the wedding. Ten days in a secluded over-the-water hut. Ten days in paradise with my new husband.

"Hey." I open my eyes to see Pierce's gaze fixed on me, a small smile playing on his lips. "We've been working hard this last year. It's about damn time we get a break."

Pierce has been working with me on my women's charity, getting it off the ground. I don't know where I'd be without him. His endless support makes me fall deeper in love with him every day.

"Before everyone gets here, I've got something for you."

"I like the sound of that." Pierce drops a hot kiss to my neck, making me forget what I'm doing.

"Stop it. Everyone will be here any minute." I shove him off of me and grab the small velvet box off the dresser.

"What's this?"

I roll my eyes. "It's a present. You need to open it." Pierce sits on the end of the bed, opening the small box.

"Love, these are beautiful." He pulls out the gold cufflinks.

"They aren't fancy or new or anything. But my granddad wore them on his wedding day, and I figured they'd be good luck. I won't tell you what else Grandmum said when she gave them to me, because I'm scarred for life."

"I'll treasure these." He closes the box and pulls me

between his legs. "Makes what I got you seem a little cheesy." He pulls a small book out of his jacket pocket.

I flip it open. Each page has a picture and a memory Pierce wrote out. Telling me why he loves me. How happy he is to be marrying me. I try to quell the tears, but they fall freely.

"Do you like it?" Pierce's voice is quiet.

"Oh, Pierce." I slant my lips over his, pouring all my emotions into this kiss. I've never been given anything so thoughtful. Pierce pulls back, wiping the tears from my cheeks.

"I'll cherish this forever." I flip through a few more pages, before setting it next to him on the bed and sitting on his lap. "I might need to go freshen up before everyone gets here now."

I revel in his handsome features. My breath catches when I see him for the first time every day. I've never felt a love like this before. To be so taken with someone, that they become your whole world. I can't imagine my life without him. He supports me in ways I never dreamed of, and I've been doing everything possible to help him adjust to royal life.

"Oy! Is anyone home?" Sean's voice carries up the stairs. I sag against Pierce, wanting just one more moment with him.

"Give us a minute!" Pierce calls down to him. "Wanker. Just letting himself in the house."

"I'm pretty sure we told everyone they could come right in after the rehearsal."

The afternoon was spent doing a walkthrough of the ceremony tomorrow. It was almost longer than the wedding itself will be. We invited our families back to our cottage for a small dinner. With how lavish everything will be tomorrow, we didn't want anything grand.

"We best get going then." Pierce drops a kiss on my lips before standing and taking my hand in his.

Pierce has been the picture of calm leading up to the wedding. I can't imagine being thrown into the public spotlight like he has and having your wedding broadcast around the globe. But he's taking it all in stride. Thinking of him by my side for the rest of our lives makes my heart flutter. I can't believe I got this lucky.

"Pierce! Charlotte! Can you believe tomorrow is the big day?" Jacqueline is in the sitting room, sipping on champagne as she comes to wrap me in a hug. Getting Jacqueline as a mother-in-law might be one of the best things about marrying Pierce.

"I can't wait to get the show on the road."

She laughs, wrapping me in her arms as Pierce takes Edward from Sean and into his arms. The love Pierce has for his nephew floors me. Seeing how good he is with him makes me anxious to start our own family. Pierce is going to be the best father in the world.

"I couldn't wait to marry Pierce's father. We were supposed to spend the night apart, but I snuck into his room." She wags her eyebrows at me.

"That doesn't surprise me." She hands me a glass of champagne, clinking her glass against mine.

"I can't wait until you're officially a part of the family."

I pull Jacqueline back in for a hug. "Not many people could handle the troubles that come along with their two sons' partners being royal."

Jacqueline cups my cheek, a warmth washing over her soft features. "Seeing how happy you make my Pierce is worth more than any troubles we might face. You two are going to have a wonderful life together."

Tears wet my eyes as I try to choke back the emotions threatening to bubble over. I sneak a peek at Pierce. He's making faces at Edward, who is giggling at his uncle. "He makes me so happy. Some days I have to pinch myself to believe this is really my life."

Jacqueline drops a kiss on my cheek. "It's going to be a wonderful life. But I wouldn't mind you popping out some more grandbabies for me. I'm not getting any younger."

I throw my head back in laughter. "That's something I can say I wouldn't mind having sooner rather than later."

"Excuse me, Jacqueline. I need Charlotte." Aunt Katherine is at my side.

"She's all yours." She pats my cheek, before I'm led over to where Pierce is talking with Sean and Ellie.

"Pierce. I need you and Charlotte so I can say a few words before dinner is served."

Pierce hands Edward back to Ellie and takes my hand, as we follow Aunt Katherine to the front of the room.

"Can I have everyone's attention for a moment?" She doesn't even have to raise her voice. When the Queen starts talking, everyone listens.

"With tomorrow being a crazy day, I want to take a moment to welcome Pierce into our family."

Pierce wraps an arm around my shoulder, pulling me in closer. His eyes are locked on Aunt Katherine as she continues.

"I know it wasn't an easy start to your relationship, and I'm afraid that's my fault. But seeing the love you and Charlotte have and the respect of duty to this country brings me great pride."

I glance up at Pierce and his eyes are wet. It wasn't an easy road for the two of us. But tomorrow, the whole world gets to see the love we have for each other.

"And as an early wedding present, I bestow the title of Duke and Duchess of Clarence on each of you."

"What?" My voice is startled. Dukedoms for married royals don't come until a few months after the wedding.

"I know I wasn't welcoming like I should have been. Pierce has been a wonderful addition to this family, and I can't wait to see how the two of you further the monarchy."

"Thank you." I wrap my aunt, the Queen, in a hug. Tears track down my face. There is no better acceptance of Pierce and our marriage than receiving this gift from the Queen.

I pull back, and she wipes the tears from my eyes. "You are such a wonderful young woman, and I couldn't be more proud of you."

My lips quiver as she wraps Pierce in a hug. Words are whispered between them that I can't hear.

Edward breaks the moment with a loud wail. "I guess we're all hungry." Ellie's eyes are wet as I look over at her and Sean. Beaming smiles radiate off everyone in the room.

"Let's give these two a moment. We'll see you in the dining room." Katherine ushers everyone out of the room, as I'm left standing in awe of what just happened.

"Did you know that was going to happen?" Pierce asks.

"It usually doesn't happen until after the wedding."

Pierce pulls me into a hug, squeezing me tight against him. I push up on my toes, peppering his face in kisses.

"I guess that means the Queen likes me." His voice is breathy as it leaves him.

I cup his cheeks, wiping a single tear that escapes. "Of course she does."

"But now I know she does. I know I don't need her acceptance, but I felt like I had to get it. Because you're worth it. And knowing she approves of me…it feels like a weight has been lifted off my chest."

"Oh, Pierce. You sweet, wonderful, kind man. I am so in love with you, it hurts some days. Never doubt that you are just the man I want you to be. Nothing more and nothing less. You're perfect."

Pierce buries his face in my neck, keeping us close together. "Christ, you have no idea how good it is to hear you say that."

"It's the truth."

Pierces kisses my neck, my jaw, my lips. "I love you more than I ever dreamed of." His smile is bright. "I have a question for you."

Laughter bubbles out of me. "And what question might that be?" We still pepper each other with questions. They're fun and lighthearted now.

"How are you feeling about tomorrow?"

"Like I'm the luckiest girl in the world."

The End

CHARLOTTE - SIX MONTHS LATER

"Charlotte! Are you home?" Zara's voice calls out through the empty palace apartment.

"In the kitchen." I sip on my tea, hating that I woke up alone this morning. The one downside of dating as a royal? Your partner can't be seen leaving your place in the morning. Pierce snuck out late last night after our date. He's only been gone a few hours, but I still miss him.

"Hi there. Wanted to drop by and tell you I won't make it to our yoga session today."

I give her a weary look. "You had to stop by and tell me that?"

She nods, grabbing a scone off the table and slathering it with jam. "I've got a few things to do today, so figured I'd pop by and see you. Plus, I had a few notes to drop off on the opening gala for the women's charity." She sets a note-card on the table in front of me. "But I best be off. Catch you sometime this week?"

Zara leans in gives me a peck on the cheek before leaving. Not wanting to waste a minute of my day, I grab the notes Zara left me but am surprised to not find the information I gave her last week, but Pierce's boxy handwriting.

MORNING CHARLOTTE.

I KNOW HOW BUSY YOU'VE BEEN LATELY WITH THE UPCOMING GALA, BUT THOUGHT YOU COULD USE A DAY TO DO SOMETHING FUN. SO GET READY – NOTHING FANCY, OF COURSE – AND I'LL SEE YOU SOON.

XX PIERCE

Just the sight of this has butterflies erupting in my stomach. There's an address at the bottom of the card. Gulping down the rest of my tea, I hurry off to my room to get ready for the day. I have no idea what he has planned for me, but knowing Pierce, it's going to be special.

Throwing on a sundress to deal with the early summer heat in London, I swipe on some mascara, lip gloss and curl the ends of my hair, wanting to look my best even if it's just me gallivanting around London today.

"Your Highness. Are you ready to leave today?" My driver, Fred, is waiting on me as I leave the palace.

"Yes. Thank you." I give him the address as he shuts the door behind me. I finger the card in my hand, tracing Pierce's words. I hate that we still have to live apart. All I want is to have him by my side when I go to bed and when I wake up in the morning. He's been keeping me going these last few weeks when planning the opening gala for my charity have threatened to drag me under.

But Pierce is there, holding my hand and planning everything with me. Even when he has his own flourishing career at Shoreditch Ink. I couldn't be more proud of him, and knowing that he's mine has a warmth spreading through me as we speed through London.

"We've arrived." I'm pulled from my thoughts as we stop in front of the restaurant. A bark of laughter escapes my lips as my door is opened.

"Princess Charlotte. We're so happy to have you here today." I'm greeted at the door before I can even take in the quirky restaurant. Boxes of cereal line the wall. Small jars of milk rest on the counter as patrons pick out their favourite cereal. "We have a small setup for you in the back if you'd like to follow up."

I smile at them, thinking of all the work Pierce put into this. Just like our first date. Where we hid away in his flat and ate the best food London had to offer.

Tucked away in a small booth are a few bowls of cereal already setup for me. "If you need anything, don't hesitate to ask."

My security officers wait off to the side as I slide in the booth. A card is resting in front of sugary cereals.

DO YOU REMEMBER OUR SECOND DATE? I WAS SO NERVOUS THAT YOU WOULD HATE EVERYTHING I PICKED OUT, THAT I BARELY REMEMBER THAT NIGHT. BUT ALL I REMEMBER WAS HOW BEAUTIFUL YOU LOOKED. AND HOW FUCKING LUCKY I WAS TO BE WITH YOU, EVEN IF WE WERE HIDDEN AWAY IN MY FLAT. BUT NOW, I'M SO PROUD TO GET TO WALK BY YOUR SIDE EVERY DAY, BECAUSE THERE IS NO ONE ELSE I WANT BY MY SIDE. ENJOY BREAKFAST. YOU'LL NEED YOUR ENERGY IF YOU PLAN TO LEARN HOW TO SCHOOL ME ON THE GOLF COURSE. XX PIERCE

My heart catches in my chest. God, this man. Sweet love notes and a hunt around London. I don't know what he has planned, but all I know is I would follow him to the ends of the Earth.

Pierce

I've checked and rechecked everything at least a dozen times. My flat is pristine. I don't think Charlotte has caught onto my plan, but it's possible she might have. I wanted the day to be special for her. To remind her how we fell in love.

The creak of the door opening has my attention jerking to the woman walking in. She looks perfectly sun kissed from a day spent in London. The dress hugging her curves leaves little to the imagination. Fuck. How did I get so damn lucky?

"Pierce? Where are you?" Charlotte shuts the door, and when her eyes take in the flat, her jaw drops in awe.

Candles cover every surface. The soft sounds of a London summer drift inside. Dinner is awaiting us in the kitchen.

"What is all of this?" Charlotte wraps her arms around my waist, pressing up onto her tip toes to give me a sweet kiss. Warm brown eyes that I love so much stare up at me.

"You've been working so hard lately, that I figured you needed a fun day." I tuck a loose strand of hair behind her ear.

"A fun day would've been spent with you." She drops a kiss to the center of my chest, and if that doesn't send my heart thumping in my chest.

"Did you have fun anyway?" I sent her all over London, visiting all the places that were special to us.

"Like a live action version of the way we fell in love." The look of love in Charlotte's eyes nearly brings me to my knees.

A smirk plays at the corner of my mouth. "I'm glad you caught on."

"Good thing I was able to answer all your questions."

"Well then." I step back from her, taking her hands in mine. "I'm hoping you're have an answer to a pretty important question." I kiss the knuckles on her delicate hand and get down on one knee.

I had a whole elaborate dinner planned out for her, but right now, Charlotte looks perfect. Glowing. Happy. Like nothing can stand in our way. No time like the present, right?

"Oh Pierce."

"Charlotte, I fell in love with you the moment you walked up to me in that park. I'd never met anyone with your passion for life. With your drive to help everyone around you. You are smart and sexy and funny, and I don't know what I did to deserve you, but if you'll let me, I'll spend every last day I'm on this Earth showing you exactly how much you mean to me."

Pulling out the box from my pocket, I open it, showing it to Charlotte. A gasp falls from her lips as she takes it in. When I asked her father for permission to marry her, he sent me straight away to the royal jeweler. I wanted the perfect ring to match the vibrant person standing before me now. With a pink diamond in the center, and a diamond sunburst surrounding it on a gold band, it fits Charlotte perfectly.

"Charlotte Jane Helena. Will you do me the great honour of becoming—"

"Yes!" Charlotte doesn't let me finish my sentence before she tackles me to the ground. "Yes yes yes!" She peppers my face with kisses as I hold her close to me.

"Thank God," I mumble against her lips.

"Were you worried?" She pulls back, her fingers tracing my jaw.

"A little. I had this perfect plan setup, and then you got here and all thought went out the window. I love you so damn much, Charlotte, that somedays it's hard to breathe."

I thumb away a tear that escapes. "I know the feeling. I never want to live a day without you, Pierce. You're all I've ever wanted, and didn't know I needed in life. I can't wait to call you my husband."

I pop the ring out of the box and slide it on her finger. Perfect.

"It's so beautiful." She eyes the ring, the light of the candles catching on the stone.

"Not as beautiful as you."

Charlotte sits up, brown hair cascading around her in a waterfall. "Is this what I have to look forward to for the rest of our lives?"

I run my hands up her thighs, taking in the sheer beauty of the woman before me. Charlotte is the most stunning woman I've ever met, and yet, it pales in comparison to the big heart she has. One she readily gave to me.

"Showering you with love? I'll never stop."

Note from the Author

Book five is now out in the world!

I fell in love with Pierce and Charlotte while writing Royal Reckoning, and just knew I had to write their book. It was a labor of love, so thank you from the bottom of my heart for reading this book!

I wouldn't be here without the support of so many people. To all the authors out there, who are too many to name… your support has made this journey one of the best I've been on! I have loved every minute of this crazy ride and only hope it continues. To my beta readers for helping to make this story perfect. Without you, I wouldn't be where I am today.

To my street team and bookstagrammers who shared and read this book…thank you! Your enthusiasm and love for my books puts a smile on my face every day.

And to all you readers who have picked up my books… thank you for taking a chance on my books. You're the best part of this journey for me!

<3 Emily

About the Author

After winning a Young Author's Award in second grade, Emily Silver was destined to be a writer. She loves writing strong heroines and the swoony men who fall for them.

A lover of all things romance, Emily started writing books set in her favorite places around the world. As an avid traveler, she's been to all seven continents and sailed around the globe.

When she's not writing, Emily can be found sipping cocktails on her porch, reading all the romance she can get her hands on and planning her next big adventure!

Find her on social media to stay up to date on all her adventures and upcoming releases!

Also by Emily Silver

The Ainsworth Royals

Royal Reckoning

Reckless Royal

Royal Relations

Royal Roots

Royal Ties

The Love Abroad Series

An Icy Infatuation

A French Fling

A Sydney Surprise

The Denver Mountain Lions

Roughing The Kicker

Pass Interference

Sideline Infraction

Illegal Contact

The Big Game

Off the Deep End — A standalone, MM sports romance

Get all my titles now:

www.ingramcontent.com/pod-product-compliance
Lightning Source LLC
Chambersburg PA
CBHW030814210726
48290CB00002B/591